Dying to take the T
Murder Mystery

Chrissie Loveday

First published 2017 by Endeavour Press Ltd.

Table of Contents

£5

Chapter One

The guide arrived at the coach depot at eight o'clock in the morning. She hid her yawns and attached a friendly smile to her face.

'Morning. I'm Demelza, reporting for duty.'

'What's your real name, love?' asked the large woman behind the counter. Probably efficient enough, she hardly looked the sort of woman who would entice her customers.

'Demelza. Yes, it really is. Demelza Price,' she added, seeing the doubt on the woman's face. 'My mum was a fan of the Winston Graham books and was determined to call me after the heroine.' She then shut up, believing she had probably said too much. The woman stared at her.

'Yes, well, it can't be helped. Nobody will believe you but it'll do for the trip. This is a new venture for the company: a tour round all the filming sites for the Poldark television series. Well, nearly all the sites. Now then, here's your passenger list. Twenty-four of them, so almost a full coach. You're booked in at Poldark Lodge and you must be there by six. Lunch is at, let me see, yes, the Sunset Café at Poltewin and that's at twelve-thirty. It's important to get to these places in good time ... not too early, though. I presume you've swotted up about all the places you're going to?'

'Oh yes. I know most of them already. I've always lived in the area anyway but I've got masses of notes.' She smiled at the woman, her dark brown eyes adding to the look of pleasure she was feeling.

'Oh dear. Don't you go reading them when you're speaking to the tour. People don't like it.'

'Oh no, of course I won't do that. It's just for myself.'

'I must say, it's a bit disappointing you don't have an accent. They'd have liked that. Still, they'll have to put up with it.' Demelza smiled. This was the first time it had ever been suggested that she should have a Cornish accent. Her parents had worked hard to stamp it out of her after she started school and began to speak like the other local children. 'Anyway, you can give me a call if you have any problems. My name is

Mabel. I really hope it all goes well. The boss of the company is relying on you to give them a good trip.'

'Okay. I'll do my best. Thanks, Mabel. I'll go and find the coach and await the passengers.'

'You'll be picking them up any minute now. I see you've got your bag with you for the overnight stay.'

'Yes, indeed. I think I'm all set to go. Thanks for your help.'

'Okay then. Off you go. Bye.' Mabel settled back to her computer and saw the girl go out of the office. She really hoped this trip would go well. It was the first of its type and the customers were paying quite a high price for their adventure. She hoped the three 'extras' they had booked all turned up at the hotel after dinner for the 'Poldark Experience' her boss had arranged. Demelza seemed fairly competent and she was pretty enough. Shame she was dark-haired and not a redhead, like the girl in the series. What was her name? Eleanor Tomlinson, that was it. She sighed and went back to her computer.

Demelza walked round the office building and saw several coaches parked there. A fairly small one had a driver sitting inside reading his newspaper. He looked up and she went towards the coach.

'Are you doing the Poldark visit?' she asked.

'That's right, love. I'm Sam, and you are?'

'Demelza. How do you do?'

'Demelza? Nice touch. So what's your real name?'

'Demelza.' She repeated her line about her mother's addiction to Winston Graham's stories and he seemed to accept it. He did have quite a wicked grin, she decided. 'So, we have to go to Bodmin, I was told.'

'That's right. Meeting everyone in the car park there. Sit in this front seat and you can tell me all about yourself as we drive.' She looked at him. He was rather nice-looking and about her own age, give or take a year or two. Blondish hair, obviously bleached by the sun. 'So, Demelza, what's your background?'

'Nothing very interesting. I had a couple of weeks off planned and saw the advert for a tour guide. I love Poldark too, so it seemed like a good plan. I was born in Cornwall and lived here most of my life.'

'What do you do? For a job I mean.'

'I work for a renewable energy company. I'm on holiday at the moment, as I said.'

'Oh wow. That's really interesting. Bit of a way from Poldark but something I'm very interested in.' He glanced at his companion. She was very pretty and had wonderful dark eyes. Very nice, he was thinking.

'So how come you're driving a coach on a trip like this?'

'Dunno really. I had a coach driving licence and saw the advert. Pretty much like you. A chance to earn a bit extra.'

'So what do you do, apart from this?'

'Well, I'm doing some research.'

'In what?'

'Oh, stuff about the ocean. Not very interesting to most people.'

'I see. I assume you're connected to some university?'

'Well yes. I'm actually working towards a PhD. Not that I tell most folk or they might think I'm being pretentious.'

'Don't know why on earth you should think that. Sounds pretty good to me.'

'I take it you've been to uni?'

'Well, yes. I did environmental science. Ecology and all that sort of stuff. Not nearly as grand as it sounds.' They drove round to the other side of the building and saw a group of folks who were standing waiting as they stopped nearby.

'Here we go. I've enjoyed our chat. Look forward to catching up some more later,' Demelza told him as she climbed down to greet her passengers. 'Good morning, all. It's a lovely day so I hope you're going to enjoy it all. I need to check your names on my list before you get on board, if that's all right. The group lined up in front of her and gave their names. 'Mr and Mrs Johnson? Right. Mr and Mrs Halliwell? Miss Watson? Miss Barker? Oh, you're together, are you?

'Yes dear. We decided to book our tickets at the same time. We do love Poldark.'

'Indeed, yes. Mrs and Mr Roderick? Fine. You can get on board now. Mr and Mrs Hardcastle? Thank you. Mrs James? Are you on your own?'

'No. I'm with Maggie ... Mrs Smith.'

'Maggie Smith? That's a famous name.'

'The actress. Yes, indeed. I usually get some funny looks when I give it.'

Demelza smiled and saw her onto the coach. She quickly read off the rest of the names. Furnival, Amos, Christopher, Leason and Quicke. That made twenty-two.

She was a couple of people short and looked around the car park to see if they were anywhere away from the rest. She got on board and asked if anyone knew the missing couple.

'No, dear. We didn't know anyone else,' said one rather large woman, nodding at her husband. He shook his head.

'We'd better wait a little while. It isn't quite quarter past nine yet. I hope you're all ready for your trip into Poldark country.' There was a general murmuring from around the coach. 'Well, my name is Demelza, yes, really. My mother had a fixation about the first series and was determined to call me that. Not sure what I'd have been if I was a boy.'

'Probably Ross,' shouted someone from the back.

'You're probably right. Our driver for the day, well, for the entire trip, is Sam, here.' He turned and gave them all a wave. 'We're planning to visit most of the sites where they filmed series one and two and some of them which are currently being filmed for series three. I hope you're all going to fall in love with some of the places and maybe even revisit them on your own. I've always lived in the area so I know it well. I know I'm very lucky and I promise, I never have and never will take it for granted. Now, any questions?'

'Yes dear. Where are we stopping for lunch?' Demelza smiled.

'At Poltewin. The Sunset Café. All included, of course. That will be at twelve-thirty. Our first stop will be on Bodmin Moor where we shall see the exterior of Ross's cottage, Nampara. Oh, here comes our missing pair. I won't say any more now until they're on board and we're on our way.'

She climbed down and went to greet the latecomers.

'Mr and Mrs Baldwin?'

'Sorry if we've kept you waiting,' said the woman, obviously an American from her accent. She was around forty and dressed in a cape and wore a fur hat. 'Our taxi didn't get to the hotel till rather late.'

'Not to worry. I'm Demelza, and once you're on the coach we'll begin our journey.'

'Demelza? Such a cute name. We do see the series back home. Bit later than you do but we love it. Being here is such a thrill. Say hi to Hermie. I hope you'll soon be firm friends. Everyone loves Hermie, don't they, love?'

'Sure thing, honey. Shall we get on board? Don't want to keep these good folks waiting any longer.' The man standing beside her looked faintly embarrassed.

Sam had climbed down to put their case in the storage beneath the coach and shut it in with the rest. They climbed on board, found seats and soon they were on their way. She picked up the microphone and began her speech.

'As I said earlier, we're starting on Bodmin Moor and St Breward. Here we shall see the exterior of Ross's cottage, Nampara. You'll see the wild country around where a lot of the shots were made of Ross and the others riding their horses. Of course, it's difficult to pinpoint actual places where they filmed but I'm sure you'll appreciate the atmosphere.' Everyone on the coach was listening avidly to everything she said.

'How exciting,' said one of the Christopher sisters.

They all got off the coach when they arrived and several of the party stood silently admiring the countryside. They were a mixed bunch of folk. The elderly Christopher sisters were both wearing matching short macs and held a somewhat old-fashioned camera. The Johnsons, a couple in their forties, were very much smarter, though the man, Wilf, was obviously in the party under sufferance. It was his wife who wanted to do the tour and he made it quite obvious. Cameras clicked as they took their photos. Back on the coach, she could hear various comments; some of them sounded slightly bored. Demelza vowed to make the next stop more interesting.

Soon they were on their way again, this time to Charlestown. Here they saw the Tall ships moored by the quay. Demelza painted a stirring picture of the port as it once was. It was featured as the principal town of Truro in the series and used for scenes of Falmouth. Everyone fell silent as they imagined the picture of crowds of men working on the ships and everyone clad in the large triangular hats, so familiar from the story.

'I expect some of you might like a coffee while we're here. I suggest we need to move on at eleven fifteen, if you prefer a bit more of a look round.' She left the party on the quayside and picked up a couple of coffees for herself and the driver.

'You're doing a great job,' Sam told her. 'Really sounding as if you knew the places well and even as though you'd been there for the filming.'

'Well, thanks. I do know the stories well so it isn't actually too difficult. I hope they're enjoying it, anyway. I told them to be back for eleven fifteen. Hope that will be enough time to get to Poltewin by twelve-thirty.'

'Should be. Then it'll be full steam ahead to Kynance and then on to some of the other places we're supposed to see.'

'Supposed to see? No question of that. We are *going* to see. Might have to get bossy if we're to pull them all in.'

Demelza counted them all back on the coach and began the next part of her story. As Sam drove them along through the lovely countryside, she talked about the stories and how Cornwall had fitted into the plot. She spoke a little about how the story was filmed, using various locations completely out of real time. She also talked about the magic of the show when it was on television and how different it was from the filming.

'For instance, remember the scene when Demelza was in the boat fishing? We were never aware of the fleet of other boats accompanying her. She looked as if she was somewhere out in the sea in the middle of nowhere. She was really in harbour at Charlestown, where you've just been. They filmed it with the open sea in the background so it couldn't be recognised. Clever stuff. The cameras, lighting and sound effects are all carried in other boats. I think it must be the editing that takes all time. I'd hate to have to do all that. But don't worry, I won't spoil any more of the story for you.'

'It's good to hear of how it was done,' said the American wife, speaking out loudly enough for everyone to hear. 'So, have you met Ross? Aidan, in person, I mean.'

'No, I'm afraid not. I'd certainly have liked to meet him. I think he's gorgeous, don't you?' A murmur of agreement came from round the bus, mostly from the women, of course. 'Though he says his first love is Seamus, of course, so unless I grow a mane and another pair of legs, there's no chance for me!'

Soon they were turning into the Sunset Café for their lunch. Sam had timed it rather well, she thought. They were five minutes early but they'd doubtless all need to visit the toilets before eating.

'There is a choice of food for you. Some of you will enjoy a hot meal and perhaps some may prefer cold food and salad. The food is part of your deal but any drinks you might want other that the tea provided, you will have to pay for, I'm afraid. Any questions? Okay, enjoy your lunch. We'll be ready to leave in about three quarters of an hour.'

The group were soon milling round in the small café and some of them rushed to the counter first, to make sure of their meals. Demelza watched, fascinated by what looked like greed to her, as some of the older ones stuffed bread rolls and butter pats into their bags. Soon they were all sitting down and eating. She spoke to Sam and suggested he should get something to eat himself.

'If you will, I will too. Come on, there's a table over there. Must say, I'm ready for something to fill this gap that's growing inside. Think I might go for fish and chips. What do you fancy?'

'I'll perhaps have a salad.'

'Very modest of you. You go and sit down. I'll bring it across for you.'

She did as she was told and looked around at her charges. Most of them seemed to be tucking in and smiling at the various other people they were sitting with. She overheard a couple of them asking if they thought her and Sam were an item. She was almost getting up to say *definitely not* but decided against that. It might be useful at some point if they thought she was in a relationship with the driver. Not that she'd have minded too much. He was definitely rather fanciable.

It was almost one-thirty by the time everyone was back on the coach ready to move on. Demelza counted them all and satisfied no-one was left behind, she told Sam they were ready.

'Excuse me, dear,' said Miss Watson, one of another pair of elderly people on the coach, 'we can't help wondering about you and Sam? I mean, are you together?' Demelza blushed, an embarrassing habit she had never quite grown out of.

'Me and Sam? No, I'm afraid not.'

'Oh, what a pity. We'd rather cast him as Ross. Sorry, I hope you don't didn't mind me asking? Only, my friend Miss Barker was wondering.'

'I don't mind at all. In fact, I'm quite flattered.' She sat down again for a few moments and then rose and picked up the microphone again.

'We're now going to drive down to the Lizard. It's the most southerly point in Great Britain and there are several places down there where the programme is filmed. I'm sure you'll recognise them when we see them. We're going to start at Gunwalloe. It's on the western side of the peninsula and we shall do a sort of loop around, after we've seen Kynance Cove. I'm sure you'll enjoy the sites as we travel round. I'll leave you in peace now and of course, I'm always ready to answer any questions.' She switched off the microphone and sat down near to Sam.

'You're pretty good at this,' he said to her.

'Well, thanks. It must come of my love for the place.'

'I know what you mean. Incidentally, I heard rumours that they are currently filming at Gunwalloe. Had you heard about it?'

'No. Nothing at all. Oh heavens, does that mean it'll all be closed off?'

'Possibly. We'll have to see. Might mean they'll get to see something of what goes on.'

'I doubt that. I've heard they completely close some areas to keep people away from the filming. I did hear that there were some distant dog walkers in one shot somewhere. Not good.'

They drove down past the Culdrose air base and she rose again to tell them all what they were seeing.

'This used to be the largest helicopter base in Europe but the Government in its wisdom decided to move the rescue service elsewhere. They have an open day each year when there are all sorts of aircraft here. It's quite a good day out. Usually held in July if anyone wants to make a date.'

They turned off the main road and drove down the narrow lane towards Gunwalloe and Church Cove. When they arrived at the car park, everyone started to talk loudly and calls of *what's going on?* were heard around the coach. Dozens of large pantechnicons were parked around the small car park.

'It looks as if they are filming on the beach,' Demelza told them. It may mean we'll be restricted in where we can go.' She opened the door to ask the man who seemed to be on guard duty what was going on.

'They're filming on the beach,' he told her. 'At least, they've just about finished. You won't be able to go on the beach at the moment. Give it half an hour and you may be able to go there.'

'Oh my goodness. Is Aidan there?' called someone from the rear of the coach, obviously excited.

'I'm afraid not, Ma'am He was here yesterday but they're just finishing off today. Background shots and so on.'

'That's so disappointing. How come you didn't know?' someone else asked Demelza, most accusingly.

'They don't actually announce these dates,' she replied feebly, keeping her fingers crossed as she told a fib. 'Well, once we've parked, you can walk along and see one of the beaches, at least. Church Cove was used as the main site for the smuggling scenes. They filmed here at night to enhance the atmosphere. You'll see it is somewhat mysterious looking and I'm sure you'll love it. You have to go through the gap over there and follow the road down to the sea.'

There was a huge buzz as everyone got off the coach and began to walk along the road. A small black tent stood at one side of the road with several actors in costume. Everyone took out cameras and began to photograph them. They played up to their audience until a steward came over to stop the people taking pictures.

'Don't stop them, love,' said one the actors. 'They only want some record of their visit.' The steward looked annoyed and said it was too late now, anyway.

'Who are you in the film?' asked Mrs Baldwin.

'Just an extra. Nobody in particular,' he replied. 'It's very boring being an extra. You sit around most of the time and leap into action at the last minute when the director calls on you.'

'Fascinating, thank you,' she said. 'Hermie, come and take a picture of the two of us together.'

'Sure thing, darling.' He snapped away on his camera and she smiled.

'Thank you so much.' The actor swept off his black hat and bowed to the party.

The party walked down to the beach at Church Cove and stood silently, imagining the action that had taken place there. It was a particularly beautiful place and most of them were first-time visitors to the county.

'What a cute little church over there.'

'I never knew Cornwall would be this lovely,' said Miss Watson. 'What's the large building on top of the cliff over there? A hotel?'

'It's an old folk's home. And if you look behind it, there's an aerial? That was the site of the first radio message across the Atlantic to America.'

13

'Oh wow, really? That must have been Marconi?' said Hermie.

'Indeed it was.'

'Lucky old folks to live there with that view,' said Miss Barker wistfully. 'It's the sort of place I'd like to live in.'

Demelza wandered along past the little church. She walked into the churchyard and looked at the graves. So many shipwrecked sailors were buried there. How sad, she thought. There was a sudden bustle of noise from the adjoining beach and people started leaving it. Stewards started removing the ropes and everyone rushed over to look at the beach. People in costumes were walking back to the car park and two crew buses drove down the road to pick up some of them.

'I can't believe the vast number of people involved,' said Mr Roderick. 'Amazing, and all for a Sunday evening entertainment.'

'I wish we'd seen Aidan,' Mrs Roderick said sadly. 'Still, we've actually seen the beach where he was filmed.'

'I like the doctor chap almost as much,' said another of the women.

'I'd settle for half an hour with any of them,' said another.

'Perhaps it's time we all got back on the coach,' suggested Demelza, with a laugh.

Chapter Two

Demelza counted them all back and told Sam they were ready to go.

'We're going to Predannack Wollas next, she announced. 'This is a rather wild, windswept headland where there were many scenes of Ross charging along on his horse. When it was filmed, there were lots of flowers out and the whole scene looked much more springlike. We shall only stop for a few minutes but long enough for you to take some pictures. Imagine Seamus charging along the top of the cliff with Ross clinging on for dear life.'

'I saw a horse box at Gunwalloe. Do you think Seamus was in there?'

'I doubt it. Probably one or two of the other horses. If Aidan wasn't there, there wouldn't be much point having his horse there,' Mr Amos spoke out.

'Oh, I am enjoying this trip,' said one of the two Misses Christopher. 'We came to Cornwall for holidays when we were little, didn't we, Marie?'

'Oh yes, but of course, it was the first Poldark series that our parents were watching at that time. I know we weren't allowed to stay up to see them.'

'We had the box set of the old series, didn't we, Wilf?' said Mrs Johnson. 'I loved it almost as much as the current series. Mind you, it's Aidan who's responsible for the current series being number one.' Wilf gave a sigh and tried to look bored.

'We can't actually get very close to the scenes but it'll give you an idea.'

'So how would they get all those vans down there? It's even narrower than the road down to Gunwalloe,' someone said.

'I don't think they did take all of the lorries down. Unless a lot of people were needed for the shots, they wouldn't really need them all. I understand they use drones to fly over and take pictures. Maybe they used them at times there.'

'He must be a good rider,' said Miss Christopher.

15

'Don't believe everything you see,' smiled Demelza. 'I do believe they used stand-ins at times. He can ride but it was a new experience to him when he got the role.' She realised how much information she had picked up when listening to his interviews.

'I said it before and I'll say it again, you're really good at this,' Sam, told her.

'Well, thanks. It's just interest that does it. And of course, I love Cornwall and have visited most places.'

'I think this is probably the closest we can get.'

'Okay. If you stop here, I'll do a bit of a spiel and we can go on the Kynance bit. Then I think it's Porthcurno and Gwenapp and by then we should be ready for Poldark Lodge.'

The rest of the afternoon was filled with lovely scenes. Most of the party were content to look over the scene from the top of Kynance and enjoyed watching the birds wheeling over and looked down on the beach. The tide was in and so the towering rocks looked as if they were right out at sea. She had to explain how different it looked at low tide when the rocks looked as if they were all on the beach and people could walk over to them. The wonderful soft white sand was covered by turquoise sea and it all looked idyllic. It was difficult to get everyone back on board to continue the trip but at last they were ready to move on.

'We have quite a long section now to get to our next stop, Porthcurno. Its main claim to fame is the theatre perched on the cliffs. It was carved out of the rocks by a lady.'

'I've seen it on television. Are we going there?'

'I'm afraid not. We don't have the time. No, we're going to look at the beach which is Nampara Cove in the series.'

'But it's miles away from the cottage,' protested Mrs Baldwin.

'This is where the television is so clever. By choosing the shots so carefully and not showing everything in the lenses, it looks as if they leave the cottage and are soon on the beach. It's a gorgeous beach with wonderful golden, soft sand.'

'Was it the one Ross and Demelza walked along in one episode?' asked Mrs Halliwell.

'I believe it was. A glorious sunny day to make Cornwall look even better.'

'Not a bad day today. We're very lucky.'

'You're quite right. We could have been wrapped up in macs and wellies. I'll be quiet for a while now so you can all relax and enjoy the countryside.'

Demelza slumped down in her seat, suddenly feeling exhausted. She still had lots to do, and leading the evening's entertainment lay ahead.

'You okay?' asked Sam.

'Fine. Just needed a few minutes.'

'Okay. I'll stay quiet and just drive.'

She closed her eyes for a few minutes and awoke suddenly to find themselves driving along the narrow lane to Porthcurno. She leapt to her feet and picked up the microphone.

'Hope you've all had a bit of a rest.' Murmurs of *yes thank you* came back to her. 'We're going to park over here and you can then walk down to the beach and enjoy seeing "Nampara Cove". It really is a lovely beach.'

'I suppose there's no chance of us going to the theatre?' asked Mrs Hardcastle.

'I'm afraid not. We have to get to our hotel. We only have just over an hour before we're due there. I'm sorry but this is a Poldark special trip and the theatre wasn't even thought of in those days.'

'What a shame. Perhaps we could come back another day.'

'That sounds like a good idea.'

'What does?' called Maggie Smith. 'I must have nodded off and missed something.'

'It's all right, dear,' her companion told her. 'Nothing missed.'

'Now, if you're ready. We have half an hour here for you to see the beach and imagine Ross and Demelza wandering along hand in hand.'

They all got off the coach and walked along to the beach. She followed them at a distance and watched to see their reaction. She giggled as the Baldwins chased across the beach towards each other, doing their Cathy and Heathcliff moment. Not quite what she'd expected but it was quite funny to watch. She noticed Maggie and her friend lingering behind the others and thought perhaps they were a little tired. It had been a long day for all of them. She went back to the coach and climbed on board.

'You all right?' Sam asked.

'Bit weary now. I think we have a break of a good hour when we get to the hotel which should give me time to revive a bit. How about you?'

'I'm fine. Like you, I'm getting there. Not much longer and we can relax for a while. Here they all come.' She rose again and fixed her smile. 'Did you all enjoy that?'

'Lovely, dear, but I hope we're going to the hotel now. I feel very weary,' Maggie told her.

'We are. It's about twenty minutes from here so you can relax and get ready for the evening's entertainment. Any questions?'

'Do we have a sea view?' asked Mr Roderick.

'I believe so. The Lodge is fairly near Gwennap Head so should have similar views. But of course, it will be dark quite soon so you won't see much till tomorrow morning. Okay Sam, I think we're all here and ready to move on.'

Poldark Lodge was a small hotel, catering for folks who wanted to be associated with the name of the television series which had re-awoken so much interest in the county. This tour had booked the entire hotel with its fifteen or so bedrooms. They were organised for the party and greeted them all with a drink. It went down well and soon they were all allocated keys for their rooms. Mrs Smith and Mrs Jones had agreed to share a room so it all worked very well. Demelza and Sam both had small rooms on the top floor so they were available for any needs the party might have. She spoke to Mrs Needham, the proprietor.

'Dinner is at seven?'

'That's right, dear. There's a choice of menu and we have a good supply of wines for them to choose from. And you have the whole hotel to yourselves. Now, I understand you'll need the television room for the evening?'

'Yes, please. And we're having a quiz and discussion. I don't suppose they'll want to stay up very late. Oh, and there are some extras coming along at some point to entertain everyone.'

'Oh yes, they did tell us that. Will they want dinner? Only, we don't have a great deal of space in the dining room.'

'I wouldn't have thought so. They're not coming till later, around eight-thirty.'

'Okay. I'll provide some coffee and a few sandwiches for them.'

'That's very good of you. Thank you. Now, if you'll excuse me, I'll go and change and freshen up for the evening.'

'Okay, dear. Hope you find everything you need.' Mrs Needham went into the kitchen to get on with preparing their evening meal. Someone tapped at the door, opened it and went into the room.

'Mrs Needham, I'm so sorry but I've locked us out of the room. We went to see the Baldwins in their room and stupidly shut the door, leaving the key inside.'

'Not to worry, love. I've got our master key. I can let you in. What number is your room? Hope you've learned your lesson,' she said with a laugh.

'It's number eight. And no worries, I'll keep the key safe in my pocket from now on.'

'Right Mr ... er? Sorry, bad of me, I know, but I've forgotten your name.'

'Johnson. Wilf Johnson.'

'Right, Mr Johnson. There we are.' She unlocked the door and he went in.

'I'll just go and tell my wife we can get in. Thanks very much.'

Mrs Needham went back downstairs and continued with her evening tasks. Typical, she thought with a smile. She nodded at another couple, wondering if she ought to issue everyone with name badges for practicality.

Back upstairs, Demelza slumped down on her bed. She felt exhausted. Silly, really, when all she'd done all day was to talk to her group. She closed her eyes and fell into a deep sleep. She awoke to hear someone knocking at the door. She shot up and looked at her watch. Heavens, it was dinner time already. It was Sam.

'You ready?' he asked.

'Sorry, I fell asleep. I must change quickly. Do you want to wait or go down?'

'I'll wait. Don't want to get ravished by one of the Misses Christopher now, do I?' She giggled.

'I think you may be safe. Wait outside and I won't take a minute.' She pulled off her trousers and top and put on a dress. She combed her hair and opened the door again.

'Good heavens. A girl who means it when she says she'll only be a minute. Where have you been all my life?'

19

'Fixing people's solar panels, no doubt. Let's go, then.' They went downstairs and joined their group in the bar.

'What are you drinking?' Sam asked.

'White wine, please. In fact, I'd better have a spritzer. Mustn't get too drunk too quickly. Still a long way to go before I can fall asleep again. Still, I do feel better.'

'Lemonade or soda water?'

'What? Oh, you mean in my spritzer. Soda, please. Lemonade makes it much too sweet. Hallo, everyone. Hope you're all ready for dinner?'

They seemed to have evolved into groups. The Johnsons were sitting with the Baldwins, the two Christopher sisters were with the other two ladies, Smith and Jones, and the Amos's and Furnivals were together. Demelza was relieved to see everyone had paired off with another couple ... the Leasons and the Quickes, the Halliwells and Rodericks and so on.

The evening was a great success, especially when the three extras arrived. Two men and one woman suddenly came into the room, threatening to kidnap Demelza. It had been agreed beforehand, as it might shock anyone else too much. Everyone laughed when Sam stood up to them and said he couldn't possibly manage without her to guide them through the rest of the trip. By half past ten, some of the group decided to go to bed. Maggie Smith was the first and her companion, Mrs James, decided to go with her. Then several of the others decided to leave as well. Soon there were only half a dozen of them left. Various men had offered to buy drinks for the two of them and Demelza was feeling somewhat weary, despite sticking to her spritzers the entire evening.

'Hermie, buy the girl a decent drink,' said his wife.

'Sure thing, honey. What can I get for you?'

'Nothing, thank you. Really. I do need to get some sleep now.'

'You sure, darling? Hermie really won't mind, will you, honey?'

'Course not. But if she doesn't want one ...'

'Okay. Okay. I get the message.'

She didn't like to leave them on their own but knew she needed to get some sleep very soon.

'I'm sorry but if I don't go to bed now, I shall be useless tomorrow. I'll see you all at breakfast. Half past eight, I believe.'

'Goodnight, honey. You have yourself a nice sleep now,' said Mrs Baldwin.

'Thank you, I will. Goodnight all.'

'Think I must go to bed, too,' Sam announced. 'Long drive tomorrow. Goodnight everyone.'

They went up the two flights of stairs and chatted outside their rooms for a few minutes.

'Give me your phone number, will you?' Sam asked.

'Course. Be nice to keep in touch.'

'I was thinking of much more than that, actually. I really like you and I'm impressed with your knowledge and abilities as a tour guide.'

'Well, thanks. You're a pretty good driver, too. Perhaps we could meet for a drink one evening? Really have a proper chat and get to know each other.'

'Sounds good to me. I must get some sleep now, however, or I shall never be up in the morning.'

'Know what you mean. Night, night then.'

'Night. Sleep well.'

Demelza went into her room and smiled to herself. She really liked Sam. He was sort of good-looking in a rugged way and had lovely eyes. A sort of greeny blue. A total contrast to herself. Her dark hair and deep brown eyes had never really appealed to her and she felt less attractive because of them. Silly really ... one was how one was. She would never have thought of interfering with any of herself with dyes or anything else. She actually wore very little makeup and preferred it that way. She brushed her teeth and finally settled down for the night. She fell asleep very quickly, realising how weary she was.

Soon the entire hotel was silent as everyone settled down for the night. The wind rose sometime in the middle of the night and then it began to rain. She woke up and cursed. This would make the trip much less appealing tomorrow if it carried on. She turned over and hoped it would blow itself out by the morning. She was just falling asleep again when a terrifying scream rang out from downstairs somewhere. She sat up, waiting for whatever would come next. She heard doors banging and someone screaming again, this time louder. She shot out of bed and grabbed her dressing gown. She went out into the corridor at the same time as Sam came out wearing his underpants.

'What the hell was all that about?' he asked.

'Don't know. I was just going to find out.'

'I'll put some clothes on and join you.'

'Good idea. Don't want to shock the natives,' Demelza replied with a nervous laugh. She almost ran down the stairs to the next floor. There she met several of the other guests trying to comfort Mrs Baldwin. 'Whatever's wrong?' she asked. A tearful Mrs Baldwin tried to speak.

'It's ... Hermie. He's –' she paused to sob ... 'he's dead.'

'Oh my goodness. What's happened?'

'She thinks he's been murdered,' Mrs Roderick told her. 'We're in the next room and she woke us with her screams.

'Okay, okay. Can you tell me what happened?'

'It's the blood. So much blood. Look, it's all on me as well.'

'It's all right. Try to calm down. Try to tell me exactly what happened.' Mrs Baldwin's sobs were still blocking everything she was trying to say.

'I woke up suddenly ... oh it was dreadful. I heard someone moving round the room.' She broke down again and cried in earnest. 'I ... I reached for the light and it wouldn't come on. Oh dear me, it was so awful.'

'It certainly sounds it.' Sam arrived at this moment so she told him what had happened.

'Oh my goodness. This was something we never bargained for.' Demelza glared at him for being insensitive.

'Go on with your story, Mrs Baldwin. You tried to put the lights on but they didn't work.'

'I leaned over to Hermie and tried to wake him. I felt something wet ... and oh my goodness, it was blood. My Hermie was bleeding. Whatever shall I do? It was horrible. Horrible.'

Mr and Mrs Needham, the proprietors of the hotel, arrived on the scene.

'What's going on?' asked Mr Needham. Demelza told him. 'Oh good heavens. I'd better call the police. Hadn't you all better go back to your rooms?'

'I'll go and make some tea for anyone that wants it,' Mrs Needham told the group.

'That's a good idea, love. I'll go and phone the police while you do it.'

'Come on, Mrs Baldwin. Come downstairs with me,' Demelza instructed. 'Sam, can you close their bedroom door? Nobody should go in.'

'If you want tea, go downstairs, and otherwise, I suggest you go back to your rooms.' He turned to close the door and realised he'd better stay there to make sure no-one went in. Perhaps there was a key he could use to lock it. Of course there was. Everyone had their own keys. He really didn't want to go inside the room and look for it, however. As soon as the company had disappeared he ran down the stairs to find Mrs Needham. 'Do you have a spare key so I can lock the room?' he asked.

'Course I do, love. Hang on a mo and I'll find it. You will bring it back to me, won't you?'

'Of course.' He stood impatiently waiting while she poured boiling water into a large teapot.

'Right. Now where did I put it?' Sam stood waiting anxiously while she shuffled through a drawer.

'It's not there. I could have sworn that's where I left it. We usually do leave it in there. Perhaps my husband's moved it, though why on earth he should I'll never know in a million years.'

'I'd better go back and stand guard till you find it,' Sam said unwillingly.

'You do that, my 'andsome. I'll send my husband up with the keys when I find them. Hasn't Mrs Baldwin got her key? Oh no, she wouldn't have it now, would she? Excuse me, I need to take the tea into the lounge to my other guests.'

Sam went back upstairs and stood outside the room, feeling as if he was on guard duty, as indeed he was. He wondered if anyone had actually looked into the room to see if Hermie really was deceased. Perhaps Mrs Baldwin had assumed it. Steeling himself, he pushed the door open and peered in. He gulped at the sight. There was blood all over the bed and the man was lying across the bed with his throat cut. Feeling somewhat sickened by the sight, Sam turned away, unwilling even to look for the keys to the room. He went out into the corridor again and met Mr Needham coming along.

'What were you doing in there?' he demanded.

'I thought I'd better check it was all as she said. Her husband is absolutely dead. His throat has been cut and, well, there's a lot of blood. Have you found the keys?'

'No, I haven't. I think they must have been stolen. We always keep them in the drawer in the kitchen. I can't think who on earth took them. And I'm not happy about you going in there,' he added.

'I was also looking to see if I could see their key. I can't stand here all night, guarding the room.'

'I'll stay here for a while. You go and get some tea.'

'Okay, thanks. What a night this is turning out to be.'

'Not good for the hotel, either. Nothing like this has ever happened before.'

Chapter Three

In the lounge, everyone was drinking tea, the universal panacea. Mrs Needham was fussing round everyone, making sure they were all supplied.

'I'll just go and make some more. Won't be a minute.' She bustled out and Sam looked for Demelza. She was in one corner, trying to get the whole story out of the deceased's wife. The rest of the party were chatting together and saying how dreadful it all was.

'You don't expect anything like this on a quiet trip round Cornwall,' Mrs Smith was murmuring.

'I don't think my husband would have let me come if he'd known this might happen,' Mrs Jones told her friend.

'I don't think mine will be too happy when he hears. What's gonna happen?' she asked Sam.

'I'm not sure. The police will want to interview everyone, I should think. I don't know how that will affect our tour.'

'It really isn't good enough,' said Mr Roderick. 'How on earth can one ever sleep peacefully in one's bed when things like this happen?'

'I'm sorry it's happened. I don't think there's any fault with the tour company's organisation, however.'

'They should have found us a secure hotel,' added Wilf Johnson. 'I shall certainly be protesting to the head office.'

'Here we are. More fresh tea,' bustled Mrs Needham.

'Bloody tea? I think we all need a brandy.' Mr Roderick turned towards the bar and went across to help himself.

'Oh, I don't know,' protested Mrs Needham, not knowing what to do. She watched as he poured himself at least a triple measure.

'Anyone else?'

Several of the men went across and took their fill. Sam gave a shrug and crossed to where Demelza was sitting.

'She's still in shock,' she whispered to him, raising her eyes towards Sadie Baldwin.

'I'm not surprised. Terrible thing to happen. Do you have any idea who could have done this?' he asked.

'Everyone loved my Hermie. Everyone who knew him. I really can't believe it.'

'I'm sure you can't. How on earth could it have happened when you were lying so close to him?'

'I woke up and realised someone was in the room. He had a torch which he shone in my eyes, blinding me. I yelled out and he fled out of the room. I then asked Hermie if he was okay and that's when I discovered all the blood. Got it all over my hands. It was awful. In fact I really need to wash and change out of my nightie. The lights didn't work and I couldn't see anyone. I think that's when I ran out into the corridor. It was terrible. I've never experienced anything like it in my life. How could anyone do that to my Hermie? He was the kindest man.'

'Now then, try to be calm. The police will be here in a while. Drink some tea and just sit quietly for a few minutes. You seemed sure it was a man who did this?'

'Oh, I don't know. Not the sort of thing a woman would do, is it?'

'Sadie, I can't tell you how sorry I am – we are,' said Mrs Hardcastle. They had been sitting with the Baldwins at one point that evening. Various others came forward with similar sentiments.

'There's nothing anyone can do at the moment. I expect the police will want to interview people tomorrow. But that's probably about it for tonight. What did they say, Mr Needham?' He had come down from his guard duty, having decided there was nothing to be gained from him staying there.

'They said they'd come here as soon as possible. That's about it, really. I suggest you all get to your beds now. I really don't know when they'll come. It must be getting on for three quarters of an hour since I called. They'll have to come from Penzance and that'll probably take 'em some time.'

Demelza felt she needed to stay with Mrs Baldwin, Sadie. The Needhams also decided to stay up with her.

'Don't worry, love. I can always get stuff ready for breakfast. I expect the police will want summat to eat as well. Fortunately we have a large freezer so I always keep a good stock of things in there,' Mrs Needham informed them all.

'I'll stay with you,' offered Sam. 'I do feel partly in charge, sort of thing. I somehow doubt we'll able to pursue much more of this tour. Will you call the operators in the morning?'

'Course I will. You go and get some sleep. No point in us both sitting here.'

'I couldn't sleep anyway. I might as well stay.'

Soon, just the three of them were left sitting in the lounge. Intermittent sobs came from Sadie, and Demelza kept comforting her, but this was becoming a little stale. The Needhams had disappeared into the kitchen and the other members of the tour had finally gone to bed. Sam heard the police arrive and went to bring them into the room.

'This is DI Blake and DC Thompson,' he announced. 'I'll leave you in their capable hands.'

'I want Demelza to stay with me,' Sadie sobbed. Then she burst into new tears and told her story yet again, sobbing as she did so.

'Can someone show me the room where it happened?' asked one of the policemen. 'Come on, Constable, let's go and take a look. The rest of you stay here.'

'I will,' offered Sam. 'As long as I don't actually have to go in there again.'

'So you have been in the room?'

'I only looked in hoping to find their key. The master key seems to have gone missing so I went to see if their key was anywhere around. It wasn't, by the way. But Hermie was lying in the bed with his throat cut. It was horrible.' He was speaking outside the lounge so Mrs Baldwin hadn't heard what he was saying.

'And you are?'

'Sam Watson. I'm the driver of the coach.'

'Okay, Sam. Lead the way. I take it you don't know any more than Mrs Baldwin has said?'

'No. Nothing more. I decided I'd better stay outside the room while everyone went downstairs. but not being able to lock the room, I went down in the end when nobody else was around. It seems the master keys have evidently disappeared too. They were kept in a drawer in the kitchen and they have gone. I wouldn't actually be surprised if they even know when they disappeared. Security is not a prime consideration here.'

'Thank you for that. Most useful.'

'This is the room. I'll leave you to it.'

Sam went downstairs again and into the lounge. The atmosphere was dreadful. Mrs Baldwin was still sobbing in one corner, with Demelza trying to comfort her and several others had come down again when they heard the police arrive. They were standing in groups, speaking quietly, obviously speculating about who was guilty. The Needhams had returned from the kitchen and were generally flapping about offering more unwanted tea and trying to clear away the used cups and saucers. He knew there was nothing he could do and went to Demelza and asked her to leave Mrs Baldwin for a moment and then suggested he might go to bed.

'But won't the police want to speak to everyone? They all seem to think so.'

'Maybe. I'm really not sure what this is going to do to our tour. Do you think we'll be able to continue?'

'Do you think they'll actually have the stamina to continue? I mean to say, if they've been up half the night, won't they be exhausted? I know I shall be, for one.'

'I'm not sure I'll even be capable of driving.'

'It's half past four now. I don't really feel as if I can leave the poor woman. Besides, the Detective Inspector did tell us to stay here.'

'I suppose so. Perhaps we should get some blankets and try to sleep.'

'I doubt I could anyway. Perhaps I should get one for Mrs Baldwin. What do you think?'

'Might give her a bit of comfort. I'll go and ask the Needhams if they have any down here.' Sam went through to the kitchen and asked if they had any blankets.

'Oh yes, of course. We should have thought of that, shouldn't we? You carry on with getting some food ready, Charlie, and I'll go and get some blankets.' Her husband nodded and put a large tray of sausages in the oven. 'Right now, my lovely, come with me and I'll find some blankets for you.' Sam followed the little woman through to a room behind the kitchen. She opened the door to reveal a stock of sheets and pillow cases and several duvets piled up on the shelves. 'There now, I knew we had some left in here from when we used to use them on the beds.' She shook out several somewhat faded blankets and passed them to Sam. 'You take them into the lounge and hand them out, will you?'

'Thank you. I'm sure they'll be welcome. Are you planning to serve breakfast sometime soon?'

'As soon as the sausages are done. In about half an hour or so, I should think.'

'That sounds great. Amazing what a disturbed night can do to the appetite.'

'Young lad like you, I bet you can eat for Britain,' she chided. 'Oh, I can hear the policemen coming down. I'd better see how they're doing and if they want some tea.' She bustled off and Sam staggered through to the lounge with his pile of blankets.

'Here you are, Mrs Baldwin, Sadie. Tuck this round you and try to relax a bit.'

'I'll never be able to sleep again. You can't imagine what it was like. Look, I still have his blood all over me.' She put out her hands to show her nightie still covered in blood.

'Perhaps we could find you something else to wear. I'll ask the policemen if we can get something.'

'Oh, I couldn't go back into that room. Not ever again. I want to go home.' She started crying again. 'This was supposed to be our trip of a lifetime. It certainly was for poor Hermie,' she murmured amidst her sobs. Demelza raised her eyebrows to Sam, as the policemen came back into the room.

'I've called for the scene of crime officers to come along. I'll be heading up the inquiry at this end but for now, I think you should go back to bed. My constable here will sit outside the room to make sure nothing is interfered with. Nobody is to leave the property until they have been interviewed. Is that clear?'

Murmurs of *yes officer* and various other chatter was heard as people rose and began to drift upstairs, led by the constable. He placed himself outside the Baldwins' room and stood there as everyone else went to find their rooms.

'I've made some sandwiches for the two of you and some tea,' Mrs Needham told the Detective Inspector. 'Shall I take them upstairs? And where would you like yours?'

'Leave them on the side table. Thank you, but I have things to do first.'

'Oh dear. I'd better tell Mr Needham everyone's gone back to bed and we won't be wanting breakfast for a while yet. I hope he hasn't started cooking bacon.' She shot off into the kitchen to sort out her husband.

'Do you want us to stay?' Demelza asked the Detective Inspector. 'Only, I've been looking after Mrs Baldwin.'

'No, you get off to bed. You might get a couple of hours before the new day gets going in earnest. I'll stay with the lady. Perhaps she'll manage to get some sleep, once I've spoken to her.' Sam nodded gratefully and left them. He needed some sleep if he was to drive later that day. Demelza was left holding the woman's hands.

'Thanks. I must say, I really could do with some sleep. I feel exhausted.' Sobs came from Mrs Baldwin as she realised her major aide was about to leave.

'Please don't leave me,' she begged.

'But the ...'

'Please don't go. You're my only friend left in the world.' A huge new bout of sobbing started from her. Demelza looked on helplessly and gazed at the policeman holding up her hands in a gesture of pleading.

'You can stay if it helps. She's obviously needing you there.'

Mrs Baldwin clung to the girl's hands as if she couldn't bear to let them go.

'Can we see if she could have a shower and perhaps get dressed?' Demelza suggested. 'Might make her feel better.'

'Good idea. I'll get my constable to collect some clothes for her. We shall need to keep what she's wearing at present.'

'Right. Oh, and please don't forget undies and something warm for her to wear. While she's doing that, I'll go and get washed and dressed myself. I'll give up on sleeping. I'd better see if there's somewhere she can have a shower.' She went through to the kitchen and asked the Needhams her question.

'Yes, my lovely, of course. She can use my shower. I'll just get her some towels. Will you bring her through?'

'Of course.'

'It's just through here. I'll show you where and you can bring her when she's ready.'

As she went back into the lounge, she was thinking about the way the tour had turned round. It had been a lovely first day and now it was all ruined. She had no idea what would happen later in the day. The police would have to interview everyone and she imagined the rest of the tour would possibly have to be abandoned. She needed to call Mabel to see what she wanted done but that would have to be later, much later. She spoke to the policeman.

'Okay. I know where she should go. Can you get her clothes?'

'Perhaps you could go and ask the constable. Tell him exactly what to look for and then you can bring them down. I'm going to call the office next and get some help out here. It's a nasty business, I must say.'

'As long as I don't have to go into the room. Hope he'll be okay with it.'

'He's an officer of the law. Well used to doing all manner of unpleasant things.' He spoke bluntly and Demelza felt a bit sorry for his colleague. She went upstairs and spoke to the constable and told him exactly what to get.

'I'm sorry. Can't be very nice for you to have to go in there.'

'Makes a change from just sitting here. But no, not a pleasant sight at all. Where do I look for everything?'

'I suppose in the wardrobe and drawers. Assuming they did unpack. Otherwise, in a suitcase? I don't think there'll be a lot of choice. They're only here for one night anyway.'

'Okay. I'll take a look. You wait out here.'

She watched him go into the dreaded room. Must be awful for the proprietors to have to clear everything out after such an event. The man's blood would have soaked into the mattress as well as the sheets and duvet. She wondered if they would be able to claim compensation from anyone. Or possibly they'd have insurance. Suddenly, she was wearied by the whole events and longed to get back to her normal job of fixing solar panels. What had seemed like a perfect holiday job had now gone sour.

'Right, love, I've got some undies and a sort of suit. Will that do?' She quickly looked over the assortment of things he'd brought out and nodded.

'I should think so. Thanks. Have you had some sandwiches?'

'Think the boss's forgotten about me. I'd love a cuppa at least.'

'I'll see what I can do. Thanks for this lot.'

'No worries.' He sat down again and pulled out his phone and began to play a game on it. She went down and took the clothes into the lounge.

'Will this do for you, Mrs Baldwin?' she asked.

'I should be wearing black.'

'I know, but this is what the constable could find. I'm sure it'll be fine for you. Come on, I'll show you where you can go to shower.' The trembling woman rose to her feet and was led through to the Needhams' private shower.

'I've put you a couple of towels ready and there's shampoo and soap there. Plenty of hot water for you, too. Hope it's all okay for you.'

'Thank you very much,' Demelza said gratefully. 'I'm going to get a shower myself now and get dressed. Oh, and the officer who is guarding the room would love a cuppa.'

'Don't leave me alone,' Mrs Baldwin begged.

'I'm here within reach,' Mrs Needham told her. 'You'll be fine. You go and change, dear. Poor thing, you must be frozen. I'll see the policeman gets his tea, don't you worry.'

The officer appeared with a large plastic bag for Mrs Baldwin's clothes and left it outside the door.

'I'll tell her to put everything in there. And thanks, Mrs Needham. You're very kind.' Demelza left the two of them and went up to her room. Sam had evidently gone to bed and she could hear him snoring away. He must have fallen asleep instantly. She had a quick shower and dressed in what she thought of as her uniform trousers and shirt. She put on a cardigan as she was now feeling rather cold. With a sigh, she glanced longingly at her bed and shut the door and went downstairs again. She was thinking about the people on the tour and wondering which, if any of them, could possibly be responsible for this atrocity. She found it hard to believe any of them could have murdered the man, but who else could have known where he would be? Or perhaps it was the room and just his bad luck to have been in that particular room? With a sigh, she went downstairs again. The Detective inspector was waiting for her.

'Ah, Miss, er ... Demelza. You don't mind me calling you that?'

'Course not.'

'I wanted you to tell me exactly what you know about this business. What did you all do yesterday for a start?'

32

'I can give you the itinerary if it helps. Not sure quite how it can but I've got a copy of it in my room. We were looking at the places where Poldark was filmed. People are interested to see them all.'

'And how did the Baldwins fit into the party?'

'They are doing a trip round parts of Britain and wanted a way to see something of Cornwall. This tour fitted into their requirements.'

'And what exactly happened last night?'

'Well, we had dinner and a quiz and some extras from the show came round and did a piece of acting for us. Then some of us had a few drinks and then it was bed-time. For me and Sam, anyway. We'd been on the go all day and were pretty tired.'

'Then what happened?'

'I was woken by the sounds of screaming. I grabbed my dressing gown and ran downstairs. I was up on the top floor next to Sam's room. Mrs Baldwin, Sadie, was hysterical and said her husband had been murdered.'

'Did you go into the room to have a look?'

'No, of course not. I just listened to what she said and took her downstairs.'

'So you only had her word for what had happened?'

'Well, yes. Sam did go and take a look and said it was a terrible mess. Blood all over the place. But you know that from what she said.'

'And how was their relationship? From what you could tell, of course.'

'Fine. She was perhaps a bit bossy getting him to take pictures of her, which he always did anyway. They seemed quite normal to me and a bit American, too.'

'What do you mean by that?'

'Oh, I don't know. Maybe a bit brash. In your face sort of thing. But they seemed fine.'

'And what about the others on the tour? Did anyone else know the Baldwins?'

'I don't honestly think so. Well, I didn't notice anyone who knew them. They did have dinner sitting next to the Johnsons. Wilf and Patsy, their first names.'

'Right, well, you've given me something to get us started. Thank you.'

Chapter Four

By six-thirty, several more of the police force had arrived, including the scene of crime officers, the SOCOs, as they were known. Clad in white suits and plastic overshoes, they trooped upstairs to what they called the murder room. Demelza and Sadie were sitting at one side of the lounge, the woman still sobbing every few minutes and sitting quietly the rest of the time. The police had commandeered another room for their interviews so the pair had been left in peace. The other guests were gradually waking up and began to come downstairs in search of breakfast. Demelza rose to speak to them.

'What time do you think we'll be going off?' asked one of the Christopher sisters. 'Only, we do want to see the rest of the sites and need to be ready to go.'

'I really don't know,' Demelza told them. 'It's a bit too early for me to call the office. But I do know the police will want to interview everyone.'

'Oh dear me,' Jessie said in a troubled voice. 'I don't think we'll like that, will we, Marie?'

'No, not all. Are we having breakfast soon? I think with the disturbed night, I'm feeling rather more hungry than usual.'

'You're just greedy, dear.'

'I don't see why you should say that. We've paid for it and I'm ready for it now.'

'Yes, but you do sound a bit greedy.'

'I'm going into the dining room to see if there's anyone about. Aren't you coming?'

'Oh, well all right then. I wonder if Mrs Smith and Mrs Jones are around? Very nice ladies, aren't they? Perhaps we could share a table with them again.'

'If they're up, we can. Come on then ...' They left the lounge and disappeared towards the dining room. Several of the other guests went into the dining room and Demelza looked somewhat longingly after them. Sam arrived and suggested they should go and join the others.

'Are you going to come and get something to eat, Sadie?' she asked.

'Oh no, my dear. I doubt I'll ever want to eat again. Poor, poor Hermie. Who on earth could have done this dreadful thing?'

'Now then, please don't start to cry again. Why don't you come with us and get a cup of tea or coffee?'

'Can I sit with you?' she asked somewhat pathetically.

'Of course you can. Come on then.' They went into the dining room where others stood up to ask her how she was.

'Fragile,' was her only response, said with great effect.

'You sit there and I'll get some coffee for you. Or do you prefer tea?'

'Coffee, please.'

'Will you have something cooked? Eggs perhaps, or maybe something more substantial?'

'Oh, no thanks, love. Nothing to eat. It would stick in my throat.' She sobbed again as she thought of Hermie's throat.

'Come on, sit down and I'll get some coffee for you.'

She was led to a table where she slumped down. Sam sat down too, looking somewhat awkward. Demelza felt totally exhausted, having coped with the woman since she was woken by her screams. She knew it was a dreadful experience for her, but surely she must stop crying soon, wouldn't she? Mrs Needham came in carrying two plates of cooked breakfast which she gave to the Misses Christopher and then came over to their table.

'I'll get you a cooked breakfast each, shall I?'

'Not for me. I'll never eat again,' moaned Sadie.

'I'll bring you some toast, then. You can nibble on that.' She bustled out and came back minutes later with a pot of coffee and some toast. 'There you are, dearie, eat up, now. Yours won't be a minute,' she said to the other two.

The whole business seemed like a dream, or rather a nightmare. More of the group came down for breakfast, and the two people who were ostensibly in charge wondered if they'd ever manage to finish the trip.

'I'll go and chat to the police Detective Inspector. See what he wants to do and then I'll phone the office to get their advice,' said Demelza when they had eaten. Never had a full English breakfast tasted so good.

'Good plan. Shall I come with you?' he added somewhat desperately. They both looked at Sadie who was eating toast as if it was going out of fashion.

'You go, dears. I'll just nibble on a little more toast.'

'Mabel?' she said on her phone. 'We've had a disaster. One of the guests has been murdered overnight. We'll all have to stay here for interviews. I'm not sure when we'll be able to leave and even if we can finish the tour.' Mabel was almost silent for moment as the news sank into her head.

'Oh my good heavens. How dreadful. We've never had anything like that happen on our tours before. Who's been murdered?'

'The American gentleman. Hermie Baldwin. His wife's in a terrible state. Some of the other guests are anxious to know what's going to happen.'

'Oh lord. I don't know what to say. I'll have to speak to the boss when he comes in. Dearie me. It's terrible. How did he die?'

'His throat was cut. Mrs Baldwin was in bed with him and woke up to find him dead. Someone was in the room and flashed a torch in her eyes. It was dreadful.'

'Goodness me. It sounds awful. Hang on in there. I'll speak to the boss and see what he suggests. Look, I'll call you back later when he's come in.'

'Okay. Thanks. I just wanted to put you in the picture. I'll speak to the police next and see what they say.'

The pair of them went in search of the police Detective Inspector. He was in conference with two other officers, who both nodded to them as they came in.

'Demelza and Sam. They are the organisers of this tour, as near as dammit. Demelza has been very helpful with the victim's wife so far. Where is she now?'

'Eating some breakfast. Lots of folk have now arrived for breakfast and some of them are asking what we're going to be doing this morning. I know they're anxious to continue their tour.'

'I'm sorry but that's impossible. We need to interview everyone and find out who can help us. My colleagues and I will soon be calling for everyone to come and have a conversation.'

'I see. I'm assuming you'll come and tell everyone your plans?'

'Well, yes. If they're all in the dining room, we'll come now.'

'I think most of them are anyway.' Sam had been standing silently during this conversation but he stepped forward at this point.

'They're not all there yet. Shall I go and knock on their doors and get them to come down?'

'That would be very helpful. Thank you. If they're all together it'll make it easier and quicker.'

'Glad to have something to do,' he commented as he left the room. Ten minutes later he came back and said all the rooms were now empty so everyone must be in the dining room.

'Right then. Let's go and get this show on the road.' He strode purposefully into the dining room and asked if he could have their attention. 'We need to speak to everyone in turn, to see what you noticed during the night.' There was a muttering among the group.

'We didn't know anything about it till this morning,' said Mrs Furnival.

'Very well, but we shall need to speak to everyone, as I said. I suggest you could all go into the lounge when you've finished eating and we'll call you into the other room Mrs Needham has made available to us. Is that clear?' Murmurs of *yes* came round the room.

'What time do you anticipate being finished?' asked Wilf Johnson. 'I mean to say, we've paid a considerable amount of money for this tour and if we can't continue with it, well ...'

''Of course, I do understand. But nobody knew this was going to happen.' There was a loud moan from Sadie Baldwin and she burst into a fresh bout of tears. 'I'm very sorry, Ma'am, really I am. But I'm sure you need to know who was guilty now, don't you?'

'Who could have done this to my Hermie? Everyone loved him, didn't they?' she demanded of Demelza.

'Please don't upset yourself again. Have you finished your breakfast? Would you like to come into the lounge?'

'I suppose so. I really don't think I could carry on with this tour. It's too much for me.'

'Don't worry about it. We'll sort out a taxi for you or something. Come on now. Let's go into the lounge.'

'I'll sit with her,' offered Patsy Johnson. 'We got to know each other a little over dinner last night.'

'Thank you so much,' Demelza said gratefully. She needed to be free to speak to the office again and also to reassure the rest of the people on the tour. She counted the couples round the tables. Twenty-one, including Sadie. She counted again and then tried to work out who was missing. She consulted her list tucked into her bag. It was the Quickes. Perhaps they were simply still in their room and she didn't know which one that was. She went to find Mrs Needham to ask her for her list of rooms so she could go and check.

'It's room twelve. Next to the end of the corridor upstairs. I hope they'm all right,' she said in a troubled voice. 'Shall I get Mr Needham to go up with you? I mean to say, if nobody's seen them since last night ...'

'Oh, I see what you mean. Yes, thank you then. If Mr Needham's free, of course,' she replied.

'I'll just fetch him out. He's clearing up after the breakfast rush.' She went into the kitchen to find her husband and Demelza stood waiting, getting rather more anxious. She couldn't face seeing any more dead bodies and made up her mind to send him in first.

'We still haven't found our master keys so we may not be able to get into the room. Damned nuisance. I told the wife she should have been more careful with them keys.' Mr Needham was obviously grumpy at being taken away from his kitchen duties. The pair went upstairs and along the corridor. 'Are you going to knock at the door?' he asked. She did so, calling out their names as she did. There was no reply. 'Best go in then, assuming the door will open.' He tried turning the handle and it opened. 'Morning,' he called out. Nothing.

'Perhaps we should put the lights on?' Demelza suggested. She reached round the door and pressed the light switch. To her great relief, nobody was in the room. The relief soon faded as she realised the implications of the Quickes being missing. 'I wonder where they are?'

'Probably gone for a walk, I should think.'

'Yes, you're possibly right. They were asking about such possibilities when I think about it.' She turned away from the room and started down the corridor.

'Interesting they've packed their things and taken their bags away,' remarked Mr Needham. She stopped and went back.

'Goodness, you're right. Why on earth would they have done that?'

'Guilty perhaps?'

'Oh no, never. Not those two. I couldn't believe it of them. I bet they wanted to get away before the police stopped them with lots of questions. Can't say I'd blame them, really. The others are getting a bit restless, I must say. Anxious to get on with the tour. I expect the Quickes must have ordered a taxi or something. I mean to say, everyone has mobile phones these days and they must have slipped away perhaps while everyone was having breakfast or something.'

'Better tell them there officers,' said Mr Needham. 'Very mysterious, isn't it?'

'It is a bit strange,' she agreed. 'But one can only speculate as to their reason.'

The Detective Inspector was a little more sceptical than the pair had been.

'How on earth can they have left? We've had people on duty outside since lord knows what time. Unless they've gone for a walk, how did they get away?'

'I'm sorry, but I don't know. They must have called a taxi or something.'

'It's a pity you couldn't have kept track of your people. Very inconvenient.'

'I think you're being a bit unfair. I was sitting with Sadie Baldwin most of the night and then I went and had a shower and well, you can't expect me to see everyone's goings on.' She felt very near to tears and began to feel angry. 'I have tried to help you as much as possible,' she finished.

'All right, I'm sorry. But you must understand it's very difficult for us to find the culprit if half of the guests go missing.'

'Only two have left. So, who do you want to see first?'

'Give me your list and I'll let you know.' She handed him the list of people without further quibble. He glanced at it and selected the first name on the list. 'I'll see Mr Johnson, please.'

'Just Mr Johnson? Not the two of them?'

'One at a time. I'll get my colleagues involved as well.'

One of the SOCOs came into the room.

'I think we're about done up in the room. The pathologist is ready for the body to be removed unless you want a further look.'

'I'll go and check what's going on. Give me a moment to organise some interviews down here and I'll join you up there.'

Demelza went back into the lounge where an anxious group went up to her.

'What's going on?' someone demanded.

'The police will want to interview everyone. Mr Johnson first.'

'What about me? I want to go with Wilf,' Patsy Johnson said.

'I'm sorry but they want us one at a time. They'll come and tell us when they're ready.'

'Why am going I first?' asked Wilf.

'They're using my list and you happened to be at the top of it. Nothing suspicious at all. Until the interviews are completed, I don't think we'll be able to leave for our tour.' There were various mutterings around the room and she heard one or two people suggesting they would want their money back. 'I'm sure you'll be compensated in some way. But you can't really blame our company now, can you?' There was a sudden wail from Sadie.

'You can't wish more than me that this had never happened. Poor Hermie.' She began to sob again and several of the women went over to her to offer their support. Demelza was grateful she was off the hook for a few moments.

It was almost nine-thirty. She spoke to Sam and they decided it was time they called the office again. There was little chance they would make it to their appointed lunch date and the office would need to let them know. She dialled the number.

'What's going on?' demanded Mabel.

'The police are still wanting to interview everyone. It seems that two of the guests have left, for some reason. Mr and Mrs Quicke. We have no idea when they went or how, even. It seems we'll be here for most of the morning. Can you let our lunch people know? I think the rest of them will want to continue with the tour when we finally get away. I was wondering if I should ask the Needhams to provide lunch. What do you think?'

'If they can, it's a good idea. But how will you fit everything in? I mean to say, there's a lot to get through before you're due back here.'

'Some of them are saying they want their money back. We'll have to do something in the way of compensation. I know it wasn't our fault, but what do I tell them?'

'Lord knows. I don't. Can't you organise something for them to do this morning?'

'I'm not sure what.'

'Oh, I don't know. A quiz or something. You've watched the programme, it shouldn't be too difficult. I'll call you when I know something or you can call me.'

'Oh dear, okay but lord knows what. You'll be willing to pay for the lunch here?'

'I suppose so. As long as I don't have to pay twice. Bye then.' She hung up. Demelza drew in her breath and went to find the Needhams.

'Course I'll do a lunch for them. Poor dears, they've really been through it, haven't they? What time would you like it?'

'Can we say midday? Can you do it in the time?'

'No worries. I'll make sure we do something. Big freezer, like I said.'

'Well thank you. I do appreciate it. You've looked after us very well.'

'We do our best, dear. I was thinking about a sort of buffet, then the police can have something if they want it. Is that all right?'

'Fine. Thanks very much. Now I'd better go and see what's going on with the interviews. Not quite what I was expecting.'

'Folks can go out into the garden if they want to. Looking quite nice out there, now the rain's stopped.'

'Thanks. Good idea. I'll let them know.'

She went back into the lounge where a few disgruntled folk were still moaning about the interruption to their planned activities. She managed to ignore their comments and looked to see who was missing. It was Wilf, obviously still being interviewed.

'Mrs Needham says you're welcome to go for a walk round the garden. She's putting together a buffet lunch, as I fear we'll still be here. Of course it will be included in the price and no extra charges will be made.' She glanced at Sam who was sitting in a corner looking bored. She crossed over to him. 'You okay?'

'Course. Pretty fed up with the situation but we just have to put up with it. Hope we can get away at some point soon.'

'You and me both.'

Chapter Five

'Well now, Mr Johnson, what can you tell us about the events of last night?' asked the Detective Inspector.

'Nothing at all. I must say, I resent being kept here. We've paid a lot of money for this Poldark trip. I never really wanted to come, but you know these women. My wife insisted.'

'I'm sorry about that, sir. But you must admit, the events of the night put a different complexion on it all. Now, I'm told you sat with the American couple for dinner last night?'

'That's right. Hermie and Sadie. They were quite entertaining. We sat with them for the evening after dinner. There were others sitting with us too.'

'And how did they seem, the Baldwins? During the evening?'

'Fine. Sadie kept asking her husband to take pictures of us. He did, of course. Several. With his phone.'

'Thank you, sir. You'd better ask to look at it, Constable,' he said, turning to ask the note taker.

'Yes sir. Shall I go now?'

'No, you can do it later. And what time did you go to bed?'

'About eleven o'clock or so. I'm not really sure.'

'And all was quiet?'

'Well yes, I suppose so. They went to their room and we went to ours. End of story.'

'I see. And what was the next thing that happened?'

'What? Oh, I see what you mean. I suppose it was when people were milling round outside our room. I went to look and see what was going on and then discovered Sadie was wailing away in the corridor. The wife came out to join us and then we went downstairs with the folks who'd come to help. Demelza and, I think, Sam were both there. We could hardly believe what she was saying. I mean to say, how could she have slept through something like that?' He sounded slightly irritated.

'Thank you, sir. And you heard nothing else? Nobody moving round?'

'Nothing. I really don't think there's anything else I can tell you.'

'Very well. That will do for now. Thank you Mr ... Mr Johnson. Could you ask your wife to come in next, please?'

'Well, I can ask her but she'll tell you nothing more than I was able to tell you.'

'If you could ask her, please, sir.' He gave an indifferent nod and left the room. 'Not the easiest of interviews. Still, someone might have heard or seen something.' The door opened and Mrs Johnson came in. 'Mrs Johnson. Please have a seat.' The woman was clearly terrified at the thought of speaking and slowly sat herself down. 'Now then, can you tell us exactly what happened to you? Starting with yesterday evening.'

'Oh well, yes. What do you want me to say?'

'I understand you sat with the Baldwins for dinner? Is that correct?'

'Oh well, yes. Yes, we did but I expect Wilf told you that. I don't know why you wanted to speak to us separately. Never mind. We'd spoken during the afternoon, on the visits, and it seemed sensible to sit with them. We all got on very well, you see. Poor Sadie. She is very upset. I didn't really like to leave her but Wilf said you wanted to see me, after him.' She looked very nervous as she twisted her hands together.

'What happened during the evening?'

'Well, we had dinner and then a sort of quiz. Then some extras came in and said they were going to kidnap Demelza. It was quite funny really. Of course, they were only playing a part.'

'Yes, indeed. And you were sitting with your new friends at this time?'

'Oh yes.'

'And what time did you go to bed?'

'We were quite late. Most of the others had already gone to bed but we were enjoying ourselves. It must have been nearly midnight by the time we went up.'

'Really? Your husband said it was about eleven.'

'Oh no. Much closer to twelve. Must have been.' She looked a bit awkward when she disagreed with something her husband had said.

'I see. The four of you stayed up together?'

'That's right. And Mr Needham, of course. I think his wife had gone to bed much earlier. He said he didn't mind us staying up. Well, we were drinking most of the time, so it made it worth his while to stay up and mind the bar.'

'I see. And what happened after that?'

'Well, I'm sure my husband told you. We woke up to the awful screaming. Sadie, you understand. I don't know how she could have slept through something like that. It's so terrible.' Mrs Johnson stopped suddenly, her eyes filled with tears and she began to sob. 'I can't believe it,' she muttered.

'I'm sure you can't. To get back to our enquiries. Who else was in the corridor with her?'

'Demelza and Sam, I think. And some of the others. The Rodericks were there. They were in the room next to them. The Baldwins, I mean. I suppose they heard her wails before anyone else.' The poor woman seemed so distressed the Detective Inspector left it at that. He didn't press her any more at this time.

'Thank you for your help, Mrs Johnson. That will do for now but we shall probably need to speak to you again later. Go and get yourself some tea or something.'

'Don't think tea will ever taste the same again.' She rose and left the room.

'She seemed quite straight, sir, didn't she?' the constable said.

'I suppose so. We'll see the Rodericks next I think. They were first on the scene.'

'Right sir. I'll go and fetch them. Er, who do you want first? Mr or Mrs?'

'Don't mind. Mrs, if she's in a fit state. The women usually give the most accurate account.'

'Right you are, sir.' He left the room and returned a moment later with a tearful Mrs Roderick.

'I'm sorry to have to do this but we need to get all the facts,' Detective Inspector Blake told her. 'Please sit down.' The woman looked terrified. 'Try to relax a bit.'

'I've never been interviewed by the police before.'

'I just need you to tell me exactly what happened. Did you speak to the Baldwins during the evening?'

'Oh yes. We all had our pictures taken by poor Hermie. Sadie, his wife, insisted. "Hermie," she said, "Take a picture of everyone. We must have something to show the folks back home." So he did. On his phone. He took pictures on his phone.'

'Pictures of everyone, you say?'

'Well, I think so. Look at his phone and see for yourself. Then the people came who were extras in the series. It was quite funny, actually. They threatened to kidnap Demelza. She took it in good part.'

'What time did you go to bed?'

'About ten-thirty. We usually go about then.'

'And what happened when you heard Sadie, Mrs Baldwin's, screams?'

'Well, we rushed out of our room to see whatever was the matter. Terrible it was. Poor woman. I can't imagine what it was like for her waking up and find him lying beside her.'

'Did you go into the room?'

'Of course not.' She gave a shudder. 'Hearing about it all was enough for me.'

'And did your husband go in?'

'Well, he looked in through the door. But no way would he go anywhere near poor Hermie.'

'So you took her words as the truth? He had his throat cut and nobody went to look?'

'Well, yes. Actually, my husband did go in and take a look and it was just as Sadie had said. Blood all over everywhere and him lying there, dead. Terrible, it was.'

'And did you hear anything? Any sounds from their room?'

'Well, no. We heard them come up to bed. Pretty late, it was. I said so to Terry. They are a bit late, I said. But then, nothing at all, not until the door was opened and she was there, wailing.' Suddenly, she began to weep. 'We never expected anything like this could happen, not in Cornwall,' she sobbed.

'It certainly is a dreadful series of events. Thank you, Mrs Roderick. Could you ask your husband to come in next. And please don't leave the premises, will you?'

'Is that all?'

The Detective Inspector nodded. 'For now anyway. We're just getting a picture of the events.'

'Thank you. I'll send Terry in then, shall I?'

'Please.' She left the room and the Constable stood by the open door, waiting for her husband. He took a few moments to come in.

'P'raps I should have gone to fetch him myself. To stop them swapping notes.'

45

'Doubt there's much they can say that will alter anything. Must say, it's a bloody awful situation. Don't see how it can have happened with nobody hearing anything. Any news on the missing couple? Quicke or Quirke or whatever their name was?'

'Shall I go and ask?'

'Wait till we've spoken to Mr Roderick. Go and see where he is, will you?'

The constable came back with Mr Roderick.

'Come in and sit down, please, sir.'

'There's nothing I can tell you that my wife hasn't said already.'

'Well, let's go through your account of what happened. Let's start with the evening.'

'There were some parlour games; Demelza was threatened jokingly and then we went to bed. That was it.'

'At what time did you go to your room?'

'About ten-thirty. Our usual time for going to bed.'

'And did you hear anything?'

'Nothing at all.'

'What about when your neighbours came to bed?'

'Didn't hear anything, like I said.'

'No comment from your wife?'

'Oh, she may have muttered something.'

'And what happened when Mrs Baldwin woke up?'

'She made a dreadful caterwauling. We shot out of bed and went to see what was wrong.'

'And did you go into the room?'

'Course not. For heaven's sake, of course I didn't.'

'Oh, but I thought you went to check that Mr Baldwin was dead.'

'Oh well, I may have looked inside. Yes, I did. But I didn't touch anything. Of course I didn't.' The man gave a shudder as he remembered his actions.

'Not a pleasant sight, I gather.'

'Not at all. But I heard nothing at all. No idea who could have done this. Do you have any idea?'

'I'm afraid not at this point. Please don't leave the premises. I may need to speak to you again.'

46

'Bad business, all this. I hope we can continue with the tour before too long. My wife will not be happy if we don't. Mind you, nor will I.'

'I'm sorry about that, sir. Thank you for your time.'

Mr Roderick left the room looking somewhat disgruntled.

'Not a lot of help, was he, sir?' the Constable commented.

'I don't know. How could anyone do this without waking anyone?'

'Perhaps we should speak to Mrs Baldwin. Could she have done it herself, do you think?'

'She's a pretty good actress if she did. But then, it could be the sort of reaction anyone might have when they did so awful a crime. I might speak to the other officers doing interviews. See if they've come up with anything.' He rose, stretching as he did so. He'd only seen four of the people so far but it seemed like forty-four, none of them very helpful. He went into the next room, knocking on the door first. 'Excuse me interrupting. Do continue.' He sat down at the back of the room and listened to his officer's interview. It was Marie Christopher who was in the room.

'I think it's a terrible thing that's happened. Terrible. I hope you discover who did it very soon so we can get on our way. My sister and I are terribly disappointed.'

'I think we all agree with your comments,' said the officer in charge of interviewing the woman. 'Unfortunately, we have to ask everyone what they heard and saw.'

'We neither saw nor heard anything,' she said firmly. 'Can I go now?' The officer glanced at Detective Inspector Blake, who nodded.

'Okay. But stay on the premises in case there's anything else to ask you.'

'Can't think what. I'm hoping we'll be leaving to complete our tour pretty soon.'

'We hope so too. Thank you, Miss Christopher.' The woman left the room looking rather angry.

'This is the trouble when there are so many of them to be interviewed. Nobody seemed to have heard anything until Mrs Baldwin started yelling. I do find it a bit strange that she didn't even wake up during the attack, don't you, sir?'

'She probably took some pills or something. I'm going to see her next, if she's calmed down a bit. Anything from any of yours?'

'Nothing at all. So far I've seen the Halliwells, Miss Watson and Miss Barker and one of the Christophers. Oh, and Mrs James.'

'Still a long way to go. See the Hardcastles next and then the Furnivals. I'll see Sadie next and we'll convene again after that.'

'Right you are, sir. Any news of the couple who went missing?'

'My constable is enquiring about that. I shall certainly want to see them. Looks very suspicious to me. Don't know where they could have gone. I'm sure if a taxi company got a call so early they'd surely have a record of it.'

'Let's hope so. Have we got the weapon yet?'

'Not yet. I suspect it may have been one of the owner's kitchen knives. But if that was the case, they'd have had to return it and clean it before putting it back.'

'Well, good luck, sir. I'll continue with my interviews, shall I?'

'Of course. I'll go and get Mrs Baldwin for interview. Let's hope she's calmed down a bit.'

Chapter Six

'Do come in and sit down, Mrs Baldwin. I hope you're feeling a little better now?'

'I'll never be the same again. Poor Hermie. What am I going to do without him? He was the world to me. We don't have a family, you see. Lots of friends, of course. They'll be so shocked. That's why we wanted so many pictures, but I'll never be able to look at them again.'

'Give it time, Mrs Baldwin. Perhaps one day you will look at them again with fond memories.'

'But they were on his phone. I don't know what's happened to his phone. It's gone missing.'

'Missing?'

'How do you know that? You haven't been back to your room, have you?'

'Well, no. But one of the men showed me his bag of things he'd taken from the room. The phone wasn't among them. I asked him specially if he'd got it and he hadn't.' The Detective inspector frowned.

'Okay. I'll look into that. Perhaps it was under the bed or something.' He doubted that completely. His officers were very thorough. He knew they'd never have missed a phone under any circumstances. 'Tell me, how well do you sleep usually?'

'Sleep? I'm a martyr to sleepless nights. I toss and turn and rarely get to sleep before it's time to get up.'

'I see. But last night you didn't hear a thing? Nobody in the room? You weren't disturbed by anyone actually murdering your husband?'

'Oh, but I took a sleeping pill last night. Knocked me out cold. Nothing could wake me when I swallow one of them. Nothing at all.' Her eyes filled with tears once again and she was about to begin sobbing again.

'I understand. So what do you think actually woke you at three-thirty last night?'

'I don't know. Perhaps it was something in my subconscious. Something told me about this terrible news. Something supernatural.

Could this have been caused by a ghost or something? I've heard so many stories about ghosts in Cornwall.'

'I don't think so. Mrs Baldwin, please try to think. You said someone flashed a light in your eyes?'

'Oh yes. They did.'

'But you couldn't see who was holding it?' She shook her head. 'Did you hear something? Someone leaving your room for instance? Perhaps you were woken when the murderer left?'

'Oh no, I don't think so. I mean to say, how do we know *when* he was murdered? It could have happened much earlier than when I woke.'

'The pathologist should be able to tell us a time when she's looked. Did you have a lot to drink last night?'

'Oh no. I never drink much. Hermie was the one who enjoyed his drinks.'

'So what did you have? A glass or two of wine with your meal? Anything afterwards?'

'We had a couple of bottles of wine with dinner. Between four of us, of course. I perhaps had a small brandy after the meal.'

'So you were feeling a bit merry?'

'It was a pleasant evening. I'd hardly say I was merry. Oh dear, I doubt I'll ever feel merry again, not without poor Hermie.' She began to cry again, in earnest. The Detective inspector looked at his constable and gave a shrug. He could see he would get nothing more out of her for a few minutes.

'I'll pause there for a few moments. Would you like some water?'

'Please. Thank you for being so considerate, officer. I feel I can't go on answering questions.'

'I'm just talking about a few moments. There are still lots of things I need to ask about. Can you get some water for her, Constable?' She flashed him a look that held pure venom but then she remembered her sobbing and went back to it. The constable arrived with some water and handed it to her. Detective Inspector Blake rose and murmured to him before leaving the room. He went to find Mr Needham.

'I understand you stayed up late last night to serve some of your guests?'

'That's right. There were four of them towards the end. The Baldwins and Johnsons. They were putting it away somewhat so I didn't mind too much.'

'And Mrs Baldwin? How much was she drinking?'

'Pretty well. She must have had about four or five brandies. Possibly more, as I had to get another bottle. I charged them for about five each, I think. And that was after at least a couple of bottles of wine. In fact, I remember I served the four of them with three bottles of one of our best wines. I didn't see how much she actually drank of them but it was a fair bit.'

'Would you say she was a bit drunk when she went to bed?'

'She obviously has a pretty good constitution. She did seem all right and thanked me for staying up with them. I wouldn't have said she seemed actually drunk.'

'I see. Thank you. So with plenty of booze and sleeping pills, I reckon she might have slept pretty heavily. Right. I'll go back to my interviews.' He went back into his interview room to find the constable standing beside the door and Mrs Baldwin still sitting, sobbing every now and then. 'Hope you're feeling better now, Mrs Baldwin.'

'I don't think I'll ever be right again.'

'I'm sure you'll recover eventually. Now then, you say you woke up and found your husband had been murdered. How soon did you fall asleep?'

'I suppose it was quite quick last night. I took my pill and, having had a drink or two, I must have dropped off pretty well right away.'

'And your husband? Did he sleep well?'

'Oh yes. Always. Never had any problems like me. He was almost asleep by the time I got into bed.'

'You were a long time after him?'

'Only a few minutes. Oh dear, my poor Hermie.' Detective Inspector Blake asked her some more questions quickly, hopefully to prevent her starting to cry again.

'Did you know any of the other members of the tour before you signed up for it?'

'No, I don't think so.' She paused for a moment. 'Actually, I know Hermie did think he recognised someone. I'm not sure who he was but he did make some comment about him. Probably something to do with money, of course.'

'I see. And how were your finances?'

'Oh heavens, I don't know. I always left all that side of things to my Hermie. He always seemed to have plenty of money.'

'How long have you been married, Mrs Baldwin?'

'Just over three years. This was a trip to celebrate the start of our fourth year together. Oh, and now it's all ruined.'

The Detective Inspector blinked. He would have thought they'd been married for considerably longer than three years. Neither of them was in the first flush of youth.

'So, what was your husband's occupation?'

'I'm not sure. Something to do with money, I think. Banking? Stocks and shares? I don't know.'

Detective Inspector Blake said nothing. He could scarcely believe that anyone married for over three years had no idea about her husband's work. He was beginning to think that Hermie's murder must also be something to do with money but it was merely a hunch.

'Okay. So think about all the people on this tour. You said Hermie thought he knew someone? Who was that?'

'I'm not really sure. He just said something like "*I didn't expect to see them on a trip like this.*" I don't actually know who he was talking about. He wouldn't say any more than that.'

'Who was he looking at when he made the comment?'

'We were getting onto the coach. He said it when we were sitting down. I've really got no idea who he was talking about. Sorry.'

'Was there anyone he wanted to speak to? To sit with? For instance, the Johnsons. You seemed to get on well with them.'

'Oh no. It was a lovely evening we spent with them.'

'How about the Quickes? They seemed to have disappeared rather suddenly.'

'It could have been, but I really don't know. It could have been anyone. Oh dear, I'm very weary now. Is there anything else you want to know?'

'We'll take a bit of a break there. I'll see you again later.'

'Thank heavens for that. I really can't answer any more questions right now.' She rose from her chair and moved towards the door. 'I'll be in the lounge with anyone who won't try to avoid me. I don't suppose they're too happy with being kept here. I must be very unpopular.'

He smiled and nodded to her. Detective Inspector Blake was feeling equally weary and frustrated at not making any real progress. The Constable said nothing, unsure of how his boss would react. He remembered how short-tempered he could be when he couldn't get the answers he wanted.

'I need some coffee,' the Detective Inspector muttered. 'How many more of these folks are there to interview?'

'I suppose there are about three couples. Maybe two. Depends on how our colleagues have got on. Shall I go and ask?'

'We'll both go. I just wish we knew who this mysterious person was that he thought he recognised.'

The other officers were finishing their interview with the Amos couple. They looked equally fed up and seemed to have got no further.

'Nothing there, sir,' he said as Mr Amos left the room.

'Mrs Baldwin suggested her husband may have recognised someone among the tourists. Any thoughts on that?'

'No-one I've seen so far. Most of them are in Cornwall for a holiday and decided to go on this tour to see something of the story, as far as I can see. One or two do live here and wanted to see the particular sights where they filmed. Wouldn't mean much to me, I must say, but my wife was always a fan. Think it was mostly because she was lusting after Aidan.'

'Aye, well, seems most of the women were like that. Right. Well, you see the Leasons next and I'll see Mrs James and Mrs Smith. Then we'll meet up to see where we're at.'

'Right you are, sir. Nasty business all round.'

'Too right. Anything found about the Quickes? I'm very suspicious of them. Perhaps you could enquire?' he told his constable.

'Right, sir. I'll go and phone the station and see if they've come up with anything.' He went outside to make his call.

'Well, have you called all the local taxi companies?' he asked. 'And none of them got a call? How the heck did they get away then?' He put the phone down and shook his head. It seemed like a complete mystery to him. The Quickes must have some reason for escaping from this place but it was miles away from anywhere. Unless is was pre-planned and someone was arranged to pick them up, he really couldn't see how they got away. Nor could he understand why ... unless it was them who were guilty of murder. It certainly seemed very likely that that could be the cause of their departure. He went back into the interview room, where Detective Inspector Blake was speaking to Mrs James.

'You're here with Mrs Smith, I understand.'

'Oh yes. I've been wanting a tour like this for ages. I live in the east of the county so it's all new territory for me. Are we going to be able to continue the tour any time soon?'

'I'm sorry, I can't say. Depends on whether we can discover who committed this terrible crime.'

'Oh dear. You surely can't think it was me?' She gave a shudder. 'I couldn't even kill one of our own hens for dinner, when it stopped laying.'

'Yes, well, I can understand that. Tell me, how do you know Mrs Smith?'

'We met at the WI. We're both members of our local group. We've been friends for about three years, it must be. They were living in America for several years and when they came back, I popped round to invite her to one of our meetings. She was delighted to join us and we've become quite close. Our husbands were never interested in Poldark, not like we are.'

'And so you decided on joining this group? Tell me, where did they live in America?' His eyes sharpened as he listened.

'I'm not sure. She'll tell you when you interview her, if you ask her.'

'Right. I may need to ask you something else later. Go and join the others now and we'll speak to Mrs Smith next. Constable, will you fetch her, please?'

'Sir,' he murmured. He returned with the woman almost immediately.

'I was wondering when it would be my turn,' she said, as she came into the room. He noticed a very slight accent ... an American accent. Could she be the person who Hermie had recognised?

'Please sit down, Mrs Smith.'

'Call me Maggie,' she told him. 'I much prefer it. Too many Smiths around, don't you agree?'

'I wouldn't know.' He decided to hit home right away. 'Did you know or have you seen the Baldwins before this tour?'

54

'Know them? I'm not sure what you mean.'

'Okay. Let's start again. Did you know Mr Baldwin before you met him on this tour?'

'Of course not.' Her eyes didn't meet his as she answered.

'Are you quite sure?'

'Look, I don't know what you're asking me. Why should you think I knew the man? America is a huge country. How on earth could I have met him before this tour?'

'But you were in America, weren't you?'

'Well, yes I was, but how did you know?'

'I just picked up a few inflections in your voice.' He smiled, feeling quite proud of himself. Not everyone could have picked up on this, he felt. But, he did admit to himself, he had been helped by her friend's comments. 'So, had you ever met Mr Baldwin previously?'

'I suppose I might have done. I did go to many conferences when I was there. Accompanying my husband, you understand. We worked together quite closely, my husband and I. But that's all in the past now. We've both retired now, you see. Come back to our old home of Cornwall, ready to start over.'

'And in what circumstances did you possibly meet Mr Baldwin?'

'Oh, I don't know. Probably we were both at the same conference. I really don't remember.'

'It sounds to me like you did know him slightly better than that. I suspect you had something in common and it upset him to see you among the members of this tour.' The woman glared at him. She looked most uncomfortable for a few moments and then drew in her breath.

'Okay. I did know him slightly. We had a battle over some real estate we both wanted to buy for our company. He wanted it too and he won, damn him.'

The Cornish police Detective Inspector was uncertain for a few moments. This was all a bit beyond his experience. Did the woman's antagonism actually stretch as far as murdering the man? He didn't really think so. He decided to take a gambol.

'Did you go into their room and did you slit his throat?' The woman paled and caught her breath.

'I certainly did not. Goodness me. How could you even think me guilty of such a crime? No, no, no. I did not kill that man.' She was so vehement in her denials that he felt she was being truthful.

Dammit, he was thinking. He'd felt sure he'd found a definite clue from someone who could have committed the crime. A few more questions and he was finished, convinced by her seemingly honest answers. He dismissed her and sat for a few minutes in silence. Apart from the two who had left, all the guests and the two tour operators had been spoken to. None of them claimed any knowledge of the murder but someone among them was not telling the truth. But who could it have been? Again he wondered if Sadie might have killed her husband but somehow, he doubted it.

The DC came back into the room.

'We've discovered Hermie's phone. It was right under the bed. And also sir, more important, we've found the knife. Again, it was right under the bed.'

'Well done. I'll look at both of them later. I'm just trying to puzzle something out.' He went back to his thoughts. He could only conclude that the two who had left, Quirke or Quicke whatever their name was, must know something. They must be found and whoever had picked them up from this remote spot, must also be found. Did he really need everyone to be kept here? He looked at his watch. It was already eleven-thirty. He decided to get his constable to make sure they had everyone's address, where they were staying in Cornwall and where their homes were. Meanwhile, he decided to have another interview with Mrs Baldwin. She had certainly been through a terrible experience but he wasn't convinced she was being completely honest.

A thought struck him. The Quickes must have given their address to the tour company. He would speak to Demelza and Sam again.

'Do you have the addresses of everyone on your tour?' he asked Demelza.

'I don't personally, but I expect they do in the office. Shall I ask them?'

'Yes, please. I want to know where Mr and Mrs Quicke have disappeared to. I really am suspicious of someone who makes a sudden exit like that.'

'It certainly was strange. They seemed okay yesterday. Didn't mix much with the rest but seemed reasonably friendly. I'll phone the office and ask them, anyway.' She went to the other side of the room and called the office. 'Hi, Mabel. Demelza here. Can you tell me the Quickes' address please? You can send it to me on the phone.'

'What's happening with you?' the woman asked.

'Nothing much. We're staying here for lunch so please make sure you cancel the other place where we were going. The police are still here and doing interviews. I think they've spoken to everyone now, except the Quickes. They disappeared in the night, hence they need their address.'

'Okay, love. Will you be able to get on with the tour, do you think?'

'I hope so. I'll let you know. Now, the address please.' She hung up and waited for a moment before the address appeared on her phone. She showed it to the police Detective Inspector.

'Oh, heavens. That's in Nottingham. I wonder where they are right now?'

'I should think they're still in the area. They haven't had time to get home yet. Sorry, it's no help to us, is it?'

'Not really. I'll make sure we've got everyone else's address and then I should think you can get off again.'

'I'll see how lunch is coming on. Thank you for your help.'

'No worries. I suppose Mrs Baldwin will want to go back to her hotel. I'll see to that. And the Needhams will want some help with clearing the room.'

'I do feel sorry for them. It's a terrible thing to have happened. Right, I'll go and see about feeding the masses.'

Chapter Seven

Mrs Needham had certainly managed a splendid buffet lunch. Amazing in so short a time, Demelza was thinking.

'That's terrific,' she told the woman. 'Thank you so much. Can I send them in now?'

'Yes, of course. My husband managed to get some salad from a neighbour and most of the rest of the stuff I had in the freezer. Amazing what one can do in an emergency.' She was slightly giggly and Demelza thought it was possibly because she was so very tired.

'Well, it all looks lovely. Thank you so much.' She went to call the tour members in for their lunch.

'I hope this isn't going to cost us anything extra,' grumbled the Misses Christopher.

'Of course not. I think Mrs Needham has done a splendid job.'

'We weren't expecting a cold lunch. Not very sustaining,' she went on.

'There are jacket potatoes and hot sausage rolls as well as sausages and the cold things. I hope that should satisfy you.' She felt annoyed with the two elderly women. She knew they'd eaten a huge cooked breakfast each. She also spotted a large quiche but decided not to say anything more. 'Enjoy this splendid lunch Mrs Needham has prepared for us. Once you've all given your addresses and contact numbers to the police Detective Inspector, I think we can get on our way again.'

'About time too,' muttered someone, whom Demelza couldn't quite identify.

'So how much of the tour will we have missed?' asked Maggie Smith.

'Hopefully, very little. We may not stay quite as long as we'd have liked but we do need to get back to Bodmin by five-thirty.'

'And what about our tea? Will we get a tea stop somewhere?' Once more it was one of the Misses Christopher.

'We can certainly make the planned tea break, Miss Christopher. Wouldn't like to think of you going hungry.'

'Really dear,' said her sister. 'You seem to think only of filling your face with something. We came to see Cornwall, not to spend most of our time feeding ourselves.'

'Oh, you are always telling me off. I don't like it.'

The two women carried on their argument as they filled their plates at the buffet. Demelza looked at Sam, who winked at her. She grinned back at him.

'Shall we go straight to Botallack and give Porthgwarra a miss?' Sam suggested.

'I think that would be a good idea. It's only a tiny place and there's much more to see at Botallack. The Levant Mine and Geevor Mines are reasonably close. We could then stop at Gurnards Head briefly. Remind me, where were we stopping for tea?'

'Along the coastal road, past Hayle and on the way to St Agnes.'

'Okay. See what the time is by then and fit in as many of the other places as we can. Pity we gave them an itinerary or they'd never know what they'd missed.'

'Knowing some of them, they'll complain about missing anything. Perhaps we can just do a whistlestop tour of the rest of the places. If we limit the amount of time they have for tea. They surely can't want much to eat. I'll give the café a call before we get there and tell them to put the kettle on.'

'Right. Well, I'm going to get myself something to eat and then we'll get on our way.'

It took nearly an hour to get everyone together and ready to move on. With the numbers depleted to twenty, it took less time to stow the luggage and say their farewells to the Needhams. Mrs Baldwin had gone with the police Detective Inspector back to her hotel in Bodmin and the Quickes were who knew where.

'Our office will be in touch with you about paying for lunch. I can't thank you enough for all your help.'

'Don't mention it, my lovely. Anyone would have done the same. Come and see us again, won't you?'

'Of course. Thank you very much.' She climbed on board the coach and picked up the microphone. 'Welcome aboard once more. I'm sorry about the delay but now we're ready to see the rest of the Poldark sites. Our next stop will be in the mining area of Botallack. Here you can see the remnants of one of the hearts of tin mining.' She spoke at length of the horrors of mining where they used dynamite to blast the rocks loose. 'Can you imagine trying to breathe with all the dust and bits of rock flying around? Death was never far away and you might remember from the series that people often died in the mines.'

'Wasn't there a disaster at Levant? I'm sure I've heard of something about it.'

'Well, yes. It was back in nineteen-nineteen. October, I think it was. Look, if you want to go and explore, I'll tell you the story as we drive along later.'

'Can we go round the mine?' asked Mr Roderick.

'I'm really sorry but we don't have enough time. You don't really have enough time to walk down to the bottom of the cliff, either. We'll need to move on soon. I'm really sorry.'

'Oh dear. That is such a pity. It looks wonderful down there.'

'Well, I couldn't manage it even if we did have time,' said Miss Watson. 'Looks very steep and unmanageable.'

Various comments came back to Demelza and she began to feel rather upset. She went back to the coach and had a moan at Sam.

'Maybe this wasn't such a good idea. I thought continuing their journey would be some sort of compensation for their morning.'

'Don't worry about it. We can only do our best and you are still doing such a great job.'

'I don't know about that. I just feel so bad about it all.'

'But they were never going to have time to go down the cliffs, were they? It was never a part of the tour. Can you imagine either Miss Christopher climbing down that path?' he laughed. Demelza giggled.

'You're quite right. Sorry, wasn't getting at you. Just having a moan.'

When they were all on board again they began to drive slowly along the dramatic cliff top. She told them about the use of this particular mine as Tressider's Rolling Mill in the series.

'Goodness, so many places have been used. They must have done so much work to make them fit into the series,' said one of the passengers.

'Oh yes. It's brought quite an economic boost to the area. Lots of people have been employed as set-builders as well as extras. We're going to drive along the coast now for quite a way. Do ask any questions you'd like to or simply enjoy the countryside.'

'You said you'd tell us about the mining disaster,' said one of the guests.

'Okay,' she began. 'You need to understand how they got down to the actual area where they were mining. Imagine huge wooden beams all strapped together for many feet to get down into the mine. Probably a couple of thousand feet in total. There were steps on these beams and the men stood on the steps as the beam moved down.'

'What, all the way to the bottom?' asked another person.

'Oh no. They got off when it started to rise again. It went up and down like a pump that drains the water out of the mine. When it came down again, they got onto the next lower steps and down to the next stopping place. Eventually it was like a long pillar of men. I think it was called a man engine.'

'So there could have been a hell of a lot of men on it by the time it got down to the bottom.'

'Oh yes. Anything up to one hundred and fifty.'

'But they weren't all killed?'

'No. There were about thirty who died, so the story goes. Something broke, maybe a bolt or something and the tower of men collapsed and fell down the mine. Can you imagine the chaos? The beam began to slip down the shaft and more and more of it broke as it took the cargo of men down with it.'

'Oh goodness. It doesn't bear thinking about,' said Miss Barker with a shudder.

'Indeed. Perhaps I shouldn't say any more.' Demelza was worried about the effect she was having on her passengers.

'Oh no, you must finish your story. You make it all seem so alive ... sorry, bad pun.'

'Okay but stop me if you don't want to hear more.' Everyone, it seemed, was gripped. 'It was several days before they got the survivors out. The death toll rose every day. The men were waiting for news, standing around the top of the site. Ladders and ropes were being used for the men to climb up. As the bodies of their colleagues were brought out from the depths of the mine, it was a case of more mourning. Some of those who had survived felt guilty and it took a very long time for them to recover. One irony was that the mine was due to have the top repaired and strengthened. There are stories told about some brave souls who stuck with the task for three or more days, not even stopping for a rest.'

'How awful. Was it the worst mining disaster ever recorded?'

'No, I don't think so. Awful as it was, there have been worse. I don't know all the details of them but there were occasions when there more deaths. On this occasion, people came from other mines around to help.'

There was silence as everyone absorbed the story.

'How do you know all this?' asked Mrs James.

'There is a website. But I've been here before and, well, I just remembered it all very clearly.' Demelza was quite moved. 'If you look at the website, there's a list of those killed. I'm sure they'll tell a somewhat different story but I think I've got the basic facts. Anyway, do relax now and enjoy the countryside.'

She slumped down in her seat, feeling exhausted both mentally and physically. She even felt near to tears at the thought of the poor men who had all so nearly been killed. In fact, the whole business of men having to go down the mines and work in such conditions made her shudder. Yet, she knew that many men regretted so many closures of mines and would have returned like a shot if the opportunity arose again.

They passed along the road, avoiding St Ives by travelling along a by-pass. It would have caused a lot of problems had they passed through the small town. They left Hayle behind them and drove along the coastal route towards the café, where they had booked for tea. Once they had finished drinking and eating, several of them wandered across the road to look at the sea and walked along the steep cliff tops. Demelza suggested to the remainder of the folks that should get on board the coach as they needed to move on.

'Is everyone back?' she asked, counting the numbers.

'The two Miss Christophers are still somewhere.'

'Oh. Perhaps they are in the toilet. I'll go and look. Sorry, Sam. Won't be a minute.' She ran back into the building and asked the assistant.

'Sorry, love. I don't think anyone is still here. I'll go and look but I don't think so.'

'Oh dear. Where on earth can they be?'

They were definitely not in the building. She went across the road to see if she could see them. There was no sign of them. She went back to the coach and asked if anyone had seen them going anywhere. No-one had.

'I saw them walking along the cliff a bit the other way,' said Mr Leason. 'They were arguing about something and waving their arms around. They looked pretty intent on where they were going.'

'Okay. Thanks. I'd better go and see if I can see them.'

'Would you like me to come with you?' offered the man.

'Well, it's up to you.' She crossed the road again and set off where Mr Leason had indicated. Several of the men had got off the coach and were following her. They walked fairly close to the edge of the cliff, looking over it. 'Be careful you don't fall,' she warned them. 'There are lots of steep places where you might trip.'

Suddenly, one of them gave a yell.

'Look. Down there.' He pointed at a body lying near the bottom.

'Oh my good heavens,' squeaked Demelza. 'That's certainly one of them, but where on earth is the other one?' They all peered over the edge but nobody could see the other Miss Christopher. 'How on earth did she fall over there? And how will we get down to her?'

'I suppose we could climb down.'

'I couldn't let anyone climb down. I'm afraid it's going to be a coastguard's job and the police, too. We'd better go back to the others and I'll phone everyone.' Her phone was still on the coach so she ran back and left them to follow her. She called 999. 'Coastguards please. Hurry. Hallo? I'm sorry but there's been an accident. One of my guests, Miss Christopher, is lying at the bottom of the cliff. I don't know where her sister is. Yes, I'm going to phone the police.' She spoke to the rest of the group who were clustered around her. 'I'm really sorry but it looks as if this ill-fated tour is at an end.'

There was inevitably a series of calls of protest which were quietened by some of them.

'Shall we go back into the café?' someone asked.

'Good idea,' said Sam. 'At least till we know what's going to happen.'

'I knew it was a bloody stupid idea to come on this tour in the first place. I hope you're satisfied now, Jean.' Mr Roderick was clearly thoroughly fed up. Poor Jean looked as if she was about to burst into tears. Wilf and Patsy and several of the others went back into the café and were holding an emergency meeting.

'Would any of you like to share a taxi back to Bodmin? The company will have to pay anyway and I don't see why we need to be kept here waiting for the bloody coastguards to rescue those dozy women. What do you say?'

'Good idea, mate. We'll share with you.' Mr Leason was more than ready. 'And I'll bet Mr Roderick will be ready to share another taxi. What about you women?'

'Oh dear, I'm not sure we should leave yet,' said Mrs James. 'What do you think, Maggie?'

'I just want to get home. So yes, I'm more than ready. Bloody fiasco it's all turned into. One murder and one accident. Quite enough deaths for one day.'

'We don't know she's actually dead yet, do we?'

'Well, maybe not. But it's unlikely anyone could have survived a fall like that. And she's getting on a bit anyway, isn't she?'

'They both are. I'm going to phone someone and see if we can't get a taxi or three,' said Wilf Johnson. 'I've had quite enough of all this nonsense.'

Demelza and Sam came back into the café. Everyone was looking very concerned and muttering together. The tour guide stood in front of the group and called for silence. Wilf Johnson was still on the phone in the corner of the room.

'Can you all listen carefully, please. Mr Johnson? This means you as well.' He put his phone down and stood silently, but actually looking furious. 'I'm afraid the police have asked that you all stay here till they have a presence. The coastguards are also on their way. Sorry, but they'll need to speak to everyone again.'

'Bloody ridiculous. If those two old bats took it into their heads to climb down the cliff, I don't see what it's got to do with any of us. Besides, a taxi is on its way to collect us and Mr and Mrs Leason. I'm sorry but I've really had enough of this Mickey Mouse operation. The firm will have to pay us for the taxi and a considerable compensation.' Wilf was in full flow and obviously very angry.

'I'm sorry, but you can't leave until the police are here and have given you permission.' Demelza was thoroughly sick of the whole tour and in many ways, agreed with him. She actually felt very close to tears after her lack of sleep during the night and with all the tension filling the place.

'Depends on who gets here first. The taxi or the police. Or my works ... oh, never mind. If the taxi gets here first, we'll be in it and on our way.'

'Let's hope it's the police and then you can argue with them.' Demelza felt everything was getting out of control. She felt helpless against all these angry men. How on earth had she ever believed this was going to be a pleasant few days? She looked at Sam for support and he stepped forward.

'You can't blame either of us for what has happened, so please stop being so angry. We are pretty fed up about it too. I suggest you either sit down and have some more tea or just sit. You have to wait for the police anyway. I know most of you are quite innocent and anxious to get on your way but please, show some respect.' Demelza looked at him and smiled weakly, so relieved to have his support.

They all went back inside and did as he had suggested. There was a buzz of angry conversation as they all took stock of the latest happening. Sam put his arm round Demelza's shoulders and whispered to her.

'I'm so sorry this has happened. Do you think one of them pushed the other over the cliff?'

'Doubt it, but it's possible, I suppose. The greedy one was constantly being told off by her sister. And someone said they were arguing as they walked along. Mind you, they often seemed to be arguing. Must be living closely with each other.'

'Well, they won't be doing that any more, I'm afraid to say. Have you phoned the office with the latest saga?'

'Lord no, I quite forgot about them. What a total shambles this tour has been.'

'You shouldn't sound so down about it. It's no fault of yours. In fact, I think you've handled it very well, despite all the moaning and complaints we've suffered. You'd better phone the office and let them know the latest. Go on, love. I'm right here beside you.'

'Thanks. Okay ... here goes.' She dialled the office number.

'Hallo?' said a weary sounding Mabel.

'Hallo. It's Demelza.'

'Oh, thank goodness. I was trying to contact you. Where are you?'

'We're parked at the tea place on the cliffs near Portreath.'

'Right. Well, stay there for a bit. Mr Kimberly will drive to find you. He wants to see everyone and try to explain what he'll do in the way of compensation.' She turned away from the phone for a moment. 'They're at the tea rooms near Portreath. Yes. I've told them to wait there. Hallo? Demelza, Mr Kimberly is on his way to meet you. Stay there till he arrives.'

'Yes, but you don't know the whole story. Miss Christopher is dead. In fact, they may both be dead. It seems they, or one of them, fell over the cliffs. The police are on their way and also the coastguards. The customers are threatening to leave and it's all such a mess.' She burst into tears of frustration. Sam leaned over and took the phone from her hand.

'Hallo? Mabel, it's Sam. I'm afraid it's true. We don't know how it happened. I don't know if it was an accident or not. They were arguing apparently, but that seems par for the course.'

'Oh my good lord. I'll just run after Mr Kimberly and tell him.' She dropped her phone and Sam heard her running out of the office. He put his hand over the speaker.

'She's run out after Mr Kimberly. He's coming over to see us and hopefully will sort it all out. Frankly, I think it's about time the office did something. Oh, hello? Did you catch him?'

'Unfortunately not. I'm going to call him on his mobile. Keep smiling, dear.' She hung up.

'Smiling? The woman's bonkers. We've got nothing to smile about.'

'Sorry. It just got all too much,' said Demelza wiping her eyes. 'I'd better have a word with the owner of this place and tell her to give everyone what they want. She'll have to bill the office.'

'Do you want something yourself?' Sam asked her.

'I couldn't. I feel so stressed out I couldn't eat or drink anything. I can't wait to get back to Bodmin and then home.'

'And that won't be for a while. By the time the police have turned up and interviewed everyone, I reckon we'll be lucky to get back much before dark.'

'Oh, don't say that. I can't bear much more of this lot. Being polite to them is just too much. Some of them are okay but if I hear any more of Wilf Johnson's moans, I might just tell him what I think of him.'

'I'll join you if you want to tackle him. We're a team, after all.'

'Oh, Sam. Thank you for being so supportive. Does my heart good to know I'm not fighting a losing battle.'

A black car drove into the car park. Everyone seemed to stand up to look at it.

'Looks like our taxi has arrived,' gloated Wilf. 'Come on, you two, let's get our luggage out of this wretched bus and we can be on our way.'

'I'm sorry but you must wait until the police arrive,' protested Demelza. 'I did tell you, you must wait.'

'And I said it depended on who arrived first. Well, it looks as if my wishes were granted. Come on, Patsy. Get moving.'

'But we do need to wait, dear. You heard Demelza.'

'You can please yourself. I'm going now. Are you coming or not?'

'Why are you in such a hurry? We're not actually due in Bodmin for another couple of hours. You'll only have to wait there.'

'For god's sake, woman. We've been messed around for long enough. Who cares about two batty old women falling over a cliff? I certainly don't. I've got nothing to say to any police that come here.'

'But you were walking along the cliffs quite near to them. I saw you. And you looked as if you were arguing with them. I saw you waving your arms about.'

'Nonsense. I was merely looking at the sea. Come on. Anyone else ready to leave this godforsaken place?'

'I was,' said Mr Leason. 'But I think we'd better stay to clear our names. Thanks all the same.'

'Please yourself. Anyone else want to come?' He looked round the group, who were all looking somewhat bewildered. 'Mrs Smith? You expressed interest.'

'I suppose I'd better stay with the rest. Tempting, I'm sure.'

'Very well. I'm on my own then. You can see to the luggage, Patsy, if you're staying here.' He went out into the car park and approached the black car. 'Hello, George. Good of you to turn out for me,' he told the driver who was sitting in his vehicle.

'Mr Johnson, it's not a problem.'

'I'm travelling on my own, it seems. Everyone else is too lily-livered to leave before the police get here.'

'Get in then, sir. We'll soon be on our way.' With a scream of tyres, he set off at a rate of knots, leaving the group standing watching.

'Oh dear,' said Patsy. 'He'll be very angry with me. Perhaps I should have gone with him.'

'You've done the right thing, dear,' said Miss Watson and she was supported by Miss Barker. 'Nobody should have left, not before the police arrived. I wonder where they are? I'd have thought they'd be here by now.'

A red car pulled up and the driver got out and came into the café.

'Taxi for Mr Johnson?' he announced.

Chapter Eight

Everyone stared at the new arrival.

'What's up? Why are you all staring at me? Where's Mr Johnson?'

Demelza stepped forward.

'I'm afraid he's just left. In a black ... car. We all thought it was his taxi.'

'Bloody hell. I've driven here from Cambourne. He said there was four of you as wanted to come. Said as how you wanted to get back to Bodmin, urgent like.'

'I'm very sorry,' Sam intervened. 'Everyone is supposed to stay here till the police arrive. They'll need to speak to everyone here.'

'Why? What's happened?'

'A dreadful accident. One lady has, well, she's fallen over the cliff and her sister is missing. So, I'm sorry but you've had a wasted journey. Oh, here come the police now,' added Demelza as she saw the police car turn into the car park. She went out to greet them. 'Thank you for coming. I've got most of the group in the café.'

'Hallo again, Miss. And where are the bodies?' asked the Detective Inspector, the same one who had spent the morning with the group at the hotel.

'We've only seen one of them. It's over the cliff over there.' She pointed over the road at the top of the spot where they'd seen Miss Christopher.

'Very well. The coastguards will be there soon. I take it, it's not a spot where anyone could climb down?'

'Oh no, certainly not. Where will you go first? Everyone's very anxious about waiting. Oh, and Mr Johnson has taken it on himself to get a taxi back. At least, we all thought it was a taxi but then another one's turned up so we don't know who the first one was.'

'And presumably his wife's gone with him?'

'No, she's still here. She's very concerned about taking her stand and staying here with everyone else.'

'Right. Well, I'll just take a look over the cliff and see what's what. Constable, you go into the café and see what going on there.'

'Right you are, sir.'

'You come with me, Miss er Demelza. Show me exactly where this problem is.' She nodded and followed him. They reached the spot and peered over.

'There she is. Down there.'

The Detective Inspector peered over and then seemed pre-occupied with looking at the ground around where they were standing. After a few hms and mutterings he turned back towards the café.

'Must get this area taped off. Step back, please. We don't want any more footprints to mess it up.' He took out his phone and dialled a number. 'Need a SOCO team out here. Yes, a load of footprints. I'm getting it taped off now. Okay.' He switched it off and Demelza stood waiting for him to say something else. 'You go back to the café. I'll be in there soon.'

They heard a motor sounding way below them and she moved forward to look. It was the inshore lifeboat coming and she sighed in relief.

'Oh, thank goodness. I couldn't bear for her to be lying there all night. Do you think her sister will be down there too?'

'That, I couldn't say. The coastguards will let us know. You go on back into the café. Try to keep them all quiet.'

'You are joking. It'll be hard to stop some of them from leaving. Especially with the taxi driver here demanding someone to drive away with him.'

'Do what you can. You say one of the men has already left?'

'Well, yes. We thought he'd gone in a taxi but then the other driver arrived and we don't know who he'd left with. Sorry, I told you that before. I don't quite know where I am or what I'm saying.'

'Take it easy, love. You've had quite a day of it.' Demelza stared at the Inspector and almost burst into tears. She swallowed hard and crunched her fingernails into her hand to stop herself.

'Thanks. It has been pretty traumatic. I'll go back into the café and try to stop anyone else from leaving.' The inspector nodded and busied himself with peering at the ground.

Everyone rounded on her when Demelza went back into the café.

'What's the news?' several of them asked.

'The inshore lifeboat is very nearly here. The Inspector has asked that you all stay here for a while. He'll be in shortly to ask what you saw.'

'I suppose I may as well go back home,' said the disgruntled taxi driver. 'If you're all staying here, there won't be any fares for me. Bloody waste of time.'

'I'd be pleased to go back with you,' said Mr Leason. 'Are you ready, dear?' he asked his wife. She shook her head.

'I don't want to upset the police. I think we should stay.'

'Okay. Anyone else?' the taxi driver asked. There were several murmurs among the crowd but no-one stepped forward. 'Right. I'm off.' He went out, looking angry and they watched him roar out of the car park. Several of the group grumbled to each other in whispers about missed chances.

The constable busied himself with speaking to various people in turn. He learned that several of them had crossed over the road to look down at the sea and one or two had even walked along the cliffs a little way. Those who had stayed inside the café were left off his inquiries. It seemed that Patsy Johnson had turned back along with the Rodericks and returned to the café.

'It was rather windy,' she explained. 'I decided it was too much for me. I don't know how far Wilf went. He did follow the Misses Christopher. I'm not saying he pushed them over but they were all arguing about something or other.'

'So where do you think he's gone to now?'

'How do I know? Bodmin, I suppose.'

'Did you recognise the car that collected him?'

'Never seen it before. I just thought it was the taxi he'd ordered.'

'Was he on the phone before he ordered the taxi?'

'Oh, you know these men and their mobiles. He'd had several calls during the day ... work related I suppose. I've long ago given up on asking who he's speaking to.'

'So you didn't hear him ordering another taxi?'

'Not at all. Not until he ordered the one that turned up. He may have ordered the other one, of course.'

'And you've no idea who the other one was?'

'None at all. Perhaps it was someone from work who came to rescue him. He didn't really want to come on this tour but I persuaded him. He really needed a break, not that it's turned into much of a break.'

'Thank you, Mrs Johnson. I'll report what you've said to the inspector.'

The constable spoke to most of the other folks and kept looking through the window to see if the inspector was coming back. The SOCO team had turned up and they all seemed to be peering at the ground. The area was now taped off and he could see the inspector looking over the cliff every now and again and then stepping back, shaking his head. At last his curiosity was raised and he went across the road to join the group.

'They've found both women. One down on the beach and the other stuck on the cliff near the bottom,' the inspector told him.

'And are they both dead?'

'Oh yes. They're putting them both in the lifeboat and taking them to Hayle. How are things back there?' he nodded towards the café.

'A lot of somewhat angry folks. It does seem as if Mr Johnson has some explaining to do, if we actually knew where he was. Who's this coming in?' They saw a new car drive into the car park. It was driven by a man wearing a smart suit and looking very officious. He strode across to the group at the top of the cliff.

'What's going on?' he demanded.

'And you are?'

'Kimberly. Owner of the tour company. Come to see what the hell's going on here.'

'I see, sir. Your tour group are mostly in the café across the road. If you'd like to join them, I'll be with you in a few minutes.'

'But what's happening? The girl said someone has fallen over the cliff. How on earth did that happen?'

'In a minute, sir. Perhaps you could accompany Mr Kimberly across to the café,' he said to the constable. 'And order me a cup of tea. I need something.'

The constable walked across to the café with the rather unwilling Mr Kimberly in tow. Demelza and Sam went over to him when they realised who he was.

'Mr Kimberly. Good to see you.'

'Are you the boss of this firm?' asked one of the men.

'Yes, indeed, I am. First let me say how sorry I am that you have had such an unfortunate tour.'

'We bloody well have. Terrible all the way.'

'Oh, that's not fair. You all enjoyed yesterday,' protested Sam. 'It wasn't until ... well, until Mr Baldwin was murdered.'

'Well, yes. Since then, it's all been terrible. I shall be demanding full recompense. We want our money back.' Several of the others agreed.

'I'll be dealing with some recompense later but you must realise that it was hardly our fault that things went wrong. And I expect you've all been enjoying meals which have to be paid for.'

'Oh yes. We've done very well, haven't we, dear?' said Mrs Barker, encouraging her friend Mrs Smith to speak.

'I suppose so,' she agreed. 'But we've been kept hanging around all morning and now most of the afternoon.'

Her American accent sounded quite strong now, thought Demelza. Interesting. Could it be her who had killed Mr Baldwin? Or was it the Quickes, who had gone missing in the night? It was all pretty mysterious and somewhat unpleasant to think about. Then, of course, there was this latest murder or possibly even murders. Somehow, it didn't seem likely that either of the Miss Christophers could have simply fallen. If only she had been more aware of where her tour members were and who they were with. She blamed herself and felt terrible about the whole business. She turned to look for Sam. He would be supportive of her but even he had disappeared. Could it possibly have been he who was guilty? After all, she had only met him for the first time yesterday and knew nothing about his background or what he really did for a living. She stopped her wild thoughts and gave a start. What on earth was she doing? Letting her imagination run wild, that's what. Sam was lovely, her every instinct told her that. He couldn't possibly be guilty of anything at all unpleasant.

It was over an hour later before they were given permission to leave. Mr Kimberly asked the Inspector in no uncertain terms to release the members of the tour. He suggested that further investigations should take place in their own homes, if necessary. There were a few cheers at this suggestion and the Inspector decided to agree.

'Please ensure your names and contact details are given to my constable and be prepared for visits from the local constabulary in your own homes. For those of you on holiday in our area, make sure we have your holiday address and your home address. And thank you all for being so patient.'

A murmuring came from the group and Demelza looked at Sam. Patience was not a word she might have used.

'Right, well, let's get back to Bodmin. It will take us about an hour or perhaps a bit more depending on the traffic. If you could all get back onto the coach when you've given your details to the constable. Thank you.'

Sam left the café and went to unlock the door of the coach. It was not quite the trip he'd expected and wondered if he'd ever be asked again to drive for the company. Pity really, as it was a nice boost to his income. He smiled as everyone came back and once they were all on board, he started the engine and began their journey back. The group seemed somewhat depleted. The Baldwins, the Christophers and the Quickes were all missing and now Mr Johnson, too.

'Are you going to give us a commentary?' he asked Demelza, quietly.

'Not really. I feel deflated and don't think there's anything more I can say. Everyone seems quieter anyway. Don't think they actually want to listen to me.'

'Maybe not. Sit back and try to relax. We'll soon be back on the A30, thence to Bodmin.'

She did as he'd suggested and sat on the single seat near to him. She closed her eyes and seemed to doze off. But her thoughts were racing round her head. So many suspects. If it was the same person who had pushed the Miss Christophers over the cliffs, it couldn't have been the Quickes. But then, perhaps it didn't have to be the same person. And Mr Johnson? Why had he been so desperate to get away? He'd even left his wife to get back home on her own. Seemed very strange.

'What are you thinking?' asked Sam.

'Nothing in particular. Everything that's happened. What a mess. I was thinking about the people who have left us.'

'Quite a few, when you think about it. What is it? Seven out of twenty-four. Seems a bit ridiculous and many miles away from Poldark. At least we know that was all fantasy. This has been a bit too near the mark.'

'You're right. It's been terrible, in fact. When I think of the optimism when we set out. Only yesterday.' They both sat silently, thinking about the loss of life. It made Demelza shudder. Who would ever have believed it could all happen on a tour of peaceful Cornwall? 'So, who do you think could be guilty?'

'I simply don't know. I do suspect Wilf Johnson.'

'Me too. It was very strange the way he was so anxious to get away. And he was the last person to be seen speaking with the Misses Christopher.'

'What do you think they were arguing about? On the cliff top back there?'

'Don't know. Surprising no-one saw him push them over though, if it had been him. You'd think someone in the group would have seen him. As I said, if he did, of course. Here we go. A30 ahead. Then straight to Bodmin.'

Chapter Nine

They arrived in Bodmin at almost the exact time they had originally planned. Everyone seemed rather subdued as they left the coach with so many unanswered questions. Three deaths hung over them all.

'Well, thank you for the time we spent yesterday. That part was good. Pity about the rest of time,' said Maggie Smith.

'I'm so sorry about everything,' Demelza said weakly. 'I'm sure Mr Kimberly will be in touch with you before too long.'

'I should bloody well think so. Proper shambles, this whole trip has been,' grumbled Mr Roderick. 'Never wanted to come in the first place.'

'It was hardly our fault,' said Sam, breaking his personal code of silence. 'We certainly didn't expect anything like this to happen. We've done our best to accommodate you all and feed you properly, so please, be reasonable.' Some of the group looked somewhat put out but they did have to agree with his words. Demelza looked grateful. 'I really don't know if the company can afford to reimburse you for the trip but I'd say the most you could expect is half a day's travel back.'

'Not good enough,' said Mr Leason. 'We've been done out of a whole lot of sights and information. Okay, we've been fed reasonably well but it wasn't what we were expecting.'

'What exactly were you expecting in the way of food?' asked Demelza.

'Oh, I don't know. Not a scratch meal like we had.'

'I really don't know how you can say that. I thought it was an excellent array of food put out at such short notice.' There were sounds of agreement from some of the others.

'Well, we missed out on over half the sights we were expecting to see today.' Mr Leason really did sound grumpy.

'I will admit that you did miss one or two places we'd intended showing you. You'll have to submit your complaints to Mr Kimberly and see what he comes up with. There's nothing we can do, I'm afraid.' Demelza turned away and got out of the bus. She and Sam went to unlock the luggage compartment and he began to lift out the cases and bags.

'Well done. I think you've spelt it out to everyone. Honestly, how they could complain about the food we got. I thought it was all excellent. The Needhams were brilliant.'

'It seems a long time ago, doesn't it? Can't believe it was only this morning we were woken by Mrs Baldwin's screams. Wonder how she's doing? Or where she actually is now?'

'We just have to leave it all to the police. No doubt they'll be in touch with everyone at some point. Oh, Mrs Leason. Which is your bag? This one, I think?'

'That's right, dear. Please don't take too much notice of my husband. He does get these flights of fancy. Nothing short of Aidan Turner arriving on site would appease him now.'

''Fraid we can't organise that one. Oh, but hang on. We do have some postcards for you all. I'd forgotten about them.' Demelza looked in her travel bag and produced a heap of cards provided by the BBC. 'Do have a couple of them. Pictures of Ross Poldark and Demelza.'

'Oh, lovely. Thank you.' She went off carrying her case and clutching her two cards.

'Pity everyone can't be as happy as that,' mused Sam. 'I hope we get paid what was agreed. Knowing this company, we might have to fight for it.'

'Surely not? We've had loads of extra work to do. I'll be furious if they try to dock our pay by even one penny.'

The rest of the tour group were waiting for their luggage by this time so the next few minutes were spent in making sure everything was collected and postcards were issued to those who wanted them. At last the bus was empty and everyone had disappeared, seemingly into the office.

'Glad I don't have to face them all,' Demelza murmured.

'Me too. I think we'll return the coach to the park round the back and wait for a while before going into the office.'

'Good plan. I'll clear out the rubbish while we're waiting.' She collected a rubbish sack and wandered along the coach picking up papers and other detritus and putting it in the bag. She stopped collecting and peered at a piece of paper she'd found under one of the seats. She stuffed it into her pocket to show to Sam later. It was probably nothing but she did wonder if it might have some clue about the events of the past day.

'You didn't really need to do that, you know,' Sam told her.

'I know. But I didn't want to have to face any more of them in the office. Look, what do you think this means?' She showed him the piece of paper.

'Don't know. Someone dropped it. Where did you find it?'

'Under where Mrs Smith was sitting. *"I'll do the job in the night if you can give me an alibi later."* Can't think what it means, unless it was related to Mr Baldwin. What has Mrs Smith got to do with it all?'

'Well, we don't know she dropped it. Not definitely. There were other folks around the same area. In fact, nobody stayed in the same seats for the whole trip. Any of them could have dropped it. And it must have been a mistake. I mean to say, something like that sounds rather mysterious, doesn't it? Somewhat incriminating, in fact.'

'Oh lord. Perhaps I should give it to the Inspector. If we do get to see him again. Trouble is, it's pretty flimsy as evidence. Maybe I should just chuck it.'

'No, don't do that. Perhaps give it in to the office? You don't need to make any accusations. We don't even know who wrote it. *"So far so good. I'll get away this afternoon. You stay quiet and you'll be in the clear."* I wonder what it means? Do you think it might have been Mr Johnson who wrote it? He's left the group, hasn't he?'

'Well, yes. I suppose so. Could he be in league with Mrs Smith in some way?' Demelza was puzzled. 'She did admit that she might have known Mr Baldwin, and Mr Johnson was very friendly with him, too.'

'But where do the Christophers fit in? I mean, both of them are now dead.'

'Maybe they accused Mr Baldwin of something?'

'What, and he was so incensed he shoved them both over the cliff?'

'Oh, I don't know. He might have done. He was seen arguing with them, wasn't he?'

'Well, yes, apparently so. But we've only got someone's word of mouth for that. It was all just an assumption. I wish he was still around. I'd like to question him myself. Really get it out of him.'

'Oh, Sam, you couldn't do that. It wouldn't be safe. If it is him who killed one or more of the people, you might be next.'

'And you wouldn't like that?' he questioned.

'Course I wouldn't.'

'That might mean you could like me?'

'Course I like you. I'd have thought that much was obvious. Come on then. Let's go to the office and see if anyone is still there.'

Sam took the rubbish bag from her and they both went round to the office. A few of the tour people were still there, arguing with Mr Kimberly. He was adamant about not giving anyone compensation at this time and told them he would be in touch when he'd sorted out payments to the various places they'd stopped for food.

'Now if you'll excuse me, I need to go and sort things out.' He turned and disappeared into a rear office, leaving Mabel trying to cope with several angry ex-passengers.

'I'll be writing to you as soon as the information is there. Now please, if you could collect your luggage and leave me alone, I'd be most grateful.'

Demelza felt sorry for the woman but couldn't add anything. Sam stood looking equally awkward and obviously wishing they'd all disappear.

'Bloody waste of time,' said Mr Leason. 'You'll be hearing from my solicitors very soon. I'm warning you.' With that threat, he turned and stormed out of the office. His wife trailed after him and they left the site. The rest of the group also decided they were getting nowhere and also left.

'Good heavens. Thought they'd never go,' said Mabel weakly. 'Sounds as if you had an eventful trip.'

'Not exactly what we were expecting.'

'Have the police said anything about who it might have been?' she asked.

'No idea. Several possibilities, of course, but nothing definite. One pair left the hotel in the middle of the night and we've no idea what happened to them. I presume you still have their home address on the books?'

'Oh yes. I've already passed this on to the police. In fact, I sent it to you. Terrible business, it all is. We never expected anything like that to happen. Poor you, having to cope with it all.'

'Well, thanks. It was all awful. I just hope it will all get sorted out and the guilty people are punished.' Demelza was beginning to feel tearful again when she thought about the ordeal they'd all suffered. She swallowed hard and put a brave face on it all. Sam smiled at her and took her hand and gave it a squeeze. She smiled back at him. 'Oh, I forgot. It may be nothing but I picked up this under one of the seats. Perhaps you can pass it on to the DI?'

'Course I will. What do you think it means?' she asked after glancing at it.

'I've no idea. Not even sure it's relevant.'

'Shall we go and have a drink somewhere? That's if you'd like to,' Sam asked.

'Thanks. I'd like that. Is there anything else you need to know?' she asked Mabel.

'Not really. We've got your contact details and you'll get your money when the accounts are completed. It shouldn't take long but there is the added complication of people demanding compensation.'

'They all ate pretty well and really only missed out on a small part of the tour, so I'm sure they can't expect all that much. Mrs Needham really came up trumps with lunch and I hope she'll be recompensed. She'll need to buy a new bed and linen too. I suppose insurance will pay for that. Horrible business.' Demelza spoke out, hoping her words would have some effect for the woman's payment.

'Yes, indeed, the Needhams were brilliant,' added Sam. 'I hope you'll look after them.' He paused and looked at Demelza, who nodded her agreement. 'Well, if there's nothing else. We'll be on our way. Bye, Mabel.'

'Goodbye, dears. Enjoy your drinks.'

'Bye,' said Demelza. It felt strangely unfinished somehow. They left together and walked across the road to a pub. 'You know, I don't really feel ready to leave. I feel as if there's something else I need to do.'

'I don't know what. But I do know what you mean. We just have to leave it to the police to sort out, don't we?'

'But there must be something else we could do or say. I suppose I don't really want to go back to my flat and return to being just me. Not with all this mystery hanging over me ... us.'

'So what do you want to do?'

'Goodness knows. I've got another week's holiday with nothing planned. Perhaps I should go away somewhere. Not sure where but it does seem such a waste.'

'And you do live in one of the main holiday areas of the country. Unless you go abroad, there's nowhere better for a holiday.'

'On my own, though? Apart from walking around somewhere, what can I do? It's not really sitting-on-the-beach weather and I visited most places, theme parks, when I was a kid. Oh, don't listen to me. I suppose it's just weariness. We haven't had a lot of sleep and the stress has been awful.'

'You're absolutely right, of course. Drink up and let's get ourselves home. I'll ring you tomorrow.'

'Thanks, that would be nice. Hope you manage to get some sleep.'

'I'm sure I will. I feel totally knackered.' They left the pub and chatted as they went to collect their cars. He reached over and kissed her on the cheek, saying goodbye as he did so.

She drove home and tried to settle. Somehow, her mind was racing around all that had happened. Someone was guilty of a brutal murder and he or she was loose in Cornwall. It didn't seem safe. She went and checked that she had locked the doors properly and put the safety chain across. She looked at it, knowing it would take much force to break the door open. She put a chair across it. At least she'd make it difficult for anyone trying to get in. Not that she really believed anyone would try to break in. She looked in the freezer for something to eat. Tomorrow she needed to go and do some shopping. She put a fish pie into the microwave and poured herself a glass of wine. She forced herself to behave normally but felt it was too hard. She didn't know why, but she definitely felt as if something unpleasant was going to happen.

'Stop being so foolish,' she said aloud. She knew she had to push bad thoughts out of her mind. She was about to sit down and eat when her phone rang. She stared at it as it persisted with its jangle.

'Hallo?' she said quietly.

'Good evening, Madam. It's Detective Inspector Black. Would it be possible for me to call round to see you? I've one or two more questions to ask you.'

'N-no. That's all right. When do you want to come?'

'In about half an hour, if that's convenient.'

'That's fine. You know where I am?'

'I have your address, of course. I'm sure we'll find you.'

'It's the ground-floor flat. I'll be waiting for you.'

Demelza gave a sigh. It was going to take ages before all this was over. She took out the pie and ate it quickly. She knocked back the wine and put the dirty glass in the sink. The doorbell rang. Quickly, she removed the chair and opened the door.

'Inspector. Oh, and Detective Thompson too. Do come in.'

'Sorry to have to bother you again.'

'Would you like a cup of coffee?'

'Yes, please.'

'No, thank you.' They both spoke together. She smiled.

'What is it to be?'

'We won't keep you. Just a couple of points to check and then we'll be on our way. You can wait for your coffee, matey.' Demelza smiled at the DC in sympathy. 'You were among the first to reach Mrs Baldwin when she woke in the night?'

'That's right. Mrs Roderick was with her. She was in the next room and was woken first.'

'Exactly who else was there?'

'Well, the others were coming out of their rooms. Several of the others. The Hardcastles came along, oh and Miss Barker. The poor Christophers also came. There were quite a group.'

'And what about the Quickes? Did you see anything of them?'

'No, not at all. They must have left soon after everyone was awake.'

'And you've no idea about where they went or why?'

'None at all. Don't you have their home address?'

'Well, yes, but they haven't turned up there. How were they during the evening before the murder?'

'A bit quiet, but they seemed to enjoy it all. They went to bed fairly early, I seem to remember.'

'Okay. Well, we'll pursue that line of enquiry. And the next question is about Mr Johnson. He left the group at the café on the way home.'

'A bit puzzling that one. He called a taxi company and then another car arrived and he left somewhat hurriedly. His wife stayed with the rest of the group. I've no idea who was in the first car but the taxi arrived later.'

'It's as we thought. Could it have been a car from his work?'

'No idea. Might have been. I'd got involved with the Christopher sisters by then. Do you think he might have pushed them over the cliff?'

'Sorry, I can't say. Was he short-tempered?'

'I suppose so, yes. He was always wanting something more to happen. He was drinking quite a lot the previous night, with the Baldwins. And then he was drinking brandy with Mr Roderick when, you know, when the murder had happened.'

'So he may have been a little drunk, shall we say?'

'He was talking normally. He didn't sound drunk at all. But I should think he was pretty used to alcohol, especially with his work. Not that I know what his work was.'

'He works for a trading company,' said DC Thomson. 'You know, stocks and shares sort of thing.' DI Black glared at him and shook his head. Demelza smiled, realising the detective had spoken out of turn.

'Well, thank you for the information. We'll probably be in touch again. You were in a privileged position as the organiser of the tour.'

'Hardly an organiser. I was just the courier.'

'All the same,' the Inspector said, 'a privileged position. Thank you again. Good evening.'

'Good evening.' She let them out and locked her door again. She even put the chair against the door as before. She really wasn't sure why she felt so nervous. As soon as it was ten o'clock, she decided to go to bed. It had been a long day ... a very long day. She fell asleep quickly. She awoke with a start and lay there wondering what had woken her. She turned over and tried to go back to sleep but heard a noise outside her window. She stiffened and her heart began to pound. Perhaps it was just a cat. She hoped it was just a cat. Her curtains were firmly closed so she could see nothing. There were no more noises and so she tried to settle again. But then, she heard a noise from the living room. She rose from her bed and crept through. Someone was definitely trying to open the catch. She was practically screaming inside and rushed through to the bedroom where she picked up her phone and dialled the police.

'Come on, come on,' she was whispering. 'Hallo? There's someone trying to break in to my flat,' she managed to say. She muttered her address. 'Please, someone come and help me.'

'They'll be there as soon as possible.' She heard a few clicks and the voice spoke again. 'I've sent instructions. They'll be with you soon. Can you shut yourself into your bathroom, say? Somewhere safe?'

'Heavens. I live in a one-bedroom flat. There's nowhere safe.'

'Try anyway.'

'Okay. I'll go there now. Please hurry. I'm so scared.'

'Is there anyone who might need to get at you?'

'Well, yes, I've been with a tour group where someone was murdered and then two others were thought to have been murdered. I'm feeling very vulnerable. Not that there's any reason for me to, but there we are.'

'Call us again if you're feeling threatened. We can stay on-line if it makes you feel better?'

'Yes, please. Then at least you'll know when they succeed to get in and possibly murder me.' Demelza ran into her bathroom and bolted the door. It was a stiff bolt as she rarely used it, living alone as she did. She flopped down onto the loo seat and waited.

Chapter Ten

There was a sudden crack and she sat there shivering. Where were the police? Who was trying to break in? In fact, had broken in?

'Demelza?' called a voice sounding gentle enough. 'Demelza, where are you?'

She was practically screaming silently as she sat shivering with terror. Whoever had killed Mr Baldwin was in her flat, ready and waiting to kill her. She crept towards the door and leaned on it as silently as she could.

'Demelza? I know you're there.' She heard them looking in her bedroom and then coming to the bathroom door. They tried to open it and rattled the door handle fiercely. 'Come on now. I only want to talk. Please come out.'

She was too terrified even to utter a word. *Please come soon,* she was praying to the police. Then she heard the sound of a police siren. Thank heavens. Whoever was at the door was suddenly silent. She heard him running back into the living room and presumed he was escaping. She heard the police banging at the door. Tentatively, she came out of the bathroom and ran to open the door.

'Oh thank goodness you're here. He's escaping through the window where he broke in.'

'Too late. He's got clean away, I'm afraid. Do you know who it was?' asked one of the officers.

'I don't know. I think it may have been the man who murdered someone last night.'

'Presumably it was a man?'

'I think so. It was only my name he called and it was said in a quiet sort of way. As if he didn't want to give anything away.'

'Did he have any sort of accent?'

'I really don't know. Oh dear. He's damaged the window catch ... well, the whole frame,' she said gazing at it in horror. 'I don't know what I can do about that.'

'We'll fix something across it. I doubt he'll be back tonight. Is there anyone we can call to come and stay with you?'

'Not really. I've been away for a couple of days and nobody knows I'm home again. I suppose there's Sam but I really don't want to disturb him. It's still the middle of the night.'

'Let's look at your window. What do you think, Harry? I reckon we'll probably have to put some screws into the side wood to hold it in place. It would work as a temporary way of holding it.'

'Maybe. But that would mean replacing the frame later.'

'Blast the man. It'll be expensive, won't it?' she said.

'Possibly. Haven't you got insurance?'

'Well, yes, but I have to pay the first lot myself and then it probably wouldn't cost much more than that. I don't have any screws, by the way. Nor any tools. Sorry, but I'm useless at anything like that.'

'What have we got in the car?'

'I'll go and look.' He went outside to the patrol car.

'Would you like some coffee?' she asked. She had now calmed down and her heart rate had reduced to something nearer normal.

'Thanks. That would be great. So, how long have you lived here?'

'About three years, I suppose. I've never had any problems like this before. It was someone who knew me. He called out my name, as I said.'

'So who do you think it might have been?'

'I was thinking it must have been the murderer. But I don't know who that was. Well, I think I might have a guess.'

'Who do you think it might have been?'

'I don't really know, but I suspect a couple of people. There's Mrs Smith, Maggie Smith or possibly Mr Wilf Johnson. I suspect it was him who may have pushed the old ladies over the cliff.'

'Hang on. Which old ladies were these?'

'Oh, two of the ladies on the tour. They fell, or were pushed over the cliffs and I've no idea why. It was really horrible. I'm sorry,' she stopped talking as tears filled her eyes.

'It's okay, love. Why don't you go and make us all some coffee?'

Demelza went into the kitchen and put the kettle on. She spooned coffee into a jug and set out three cups and saucers on a tray. She added sugar and milk and carried it through to the sitting room. Then she took the coffee jug back into the kitchen and waited for the kettle to boil, wondering what she'd been thinking of. The policeman came back inside.

'I've just had a call about someone speeding like a bat out of hell on the by-pass. They think he may have come from this area. Could be your break-in artist. Should I go and chase him? Doubt if I'll catch him now.'

'Forget it. We'd better try to make this window safe before we leave. Trouble is, plastic windows don't give you much scope to add anything without ruining them.'

'I don't care,' Demelza protested. 'Do something with it. I can't stay here with it like that. Suppose he or she comes back?'

'I doubt they will. Who's dealing with your case? CID, I mean.'

'Inspector Black and whatever he is Thompson.'

'And have you told them of your suspicions?'

'Not really. It's only since I got home and had time to think. But it really is only my suspicion. No facts to go on. Sorry, I'll make your coffee.' She busied herself with the coffee jug and carried it into the living room. 'How do you like it?'

'Two sugars and white, please.'

'Same for me, thanks.'

'Look, we've been talking. You should tell CID of your suspicions. Phone them in the morning. You could save them a lot of time. We'll let them know about this break-in anyway. They'll possibly call you.'

'Okay, I will. Thanks. I was also thinking. You can't really do much about my window. It's not all that much longer till dawn. As you say, it's not really likely whoever it was will come back. Hopefully you scared them and ... well, I'm sure I'll be all right. I can phone someone first thing to come and repair the damage.'

'That's brave of you. I agree with your thoughts. We'll need to get back to base fairly soon. If you're sure you'll be all right.'

'As sure as I'll ever be. Thanks for your concern and for coming.'

'I wouldn't mind a drop more coffee before we go,' said Harry. She smiled and poured it for him. The other officer shook his head. She saw them off and carefully locked the door again. She then sat down in the living room, staring at the broken window catch as if just looking would fix it. She dozed slightly and realised it was half past seven. She thought she could possibly call Sam and tell him about her disturbed night. She dialled the number he'd put in her phone.

'Hallo?' said a very sleepy voice.

'Sam? It's Demelza. How are you?'

'Still asleep. What time is it?'

'Half past seven.'

'Crikey. You're up early. What's up? Couldn't you sleep?'

'Someone tried to break in. Well, they got in, actually. I was hiding in the loo. Then the police arrived and the thief escaped from where he'd broken in.'

'Good heavens. Are you all right?'

'Shaken a bit. I take it you weren't disturbed?'

'Not at all. Who do you think it was?'

'Dunno. They knew my name. I reckon it might have been the person who killed Mr Baldwin.'

'Male or female?'

'Not sure.'

'I'll be over soon. Where do you live?' he asked. She gave him her address and directions. 'I'm so sorry. Don't worry. I'll be there soon.'

'Thanks. I'll be grateful. I'll make us some breakfast.'

'Are you all right?' he asked with some concern. 'A horrible thing to happen. Tell me exactly what went on.' She repeated the saga to him and agreed she needed to tell DI Black and his colleague. 'Come on. You've got his card somewhere. Let's do it right away.'

They had finished eating breakfast by now and she picked up her phone and dialled the number on the card.

'Detective Inspector Black,' the voice said.

'Hallo. This is Demelza Price, from the Poldark trip.'

'Yes, of course. What can I do for you?'

'I had a break-in last night.'

'Really? Who was it? Do you know?'

'I don't know for sure but I'm suspicious it might have been the murderer. There was a voice that called out my name so they obviously knew where they were going. I called the police and they came and the burglar escaped.'

'You say "burglar" and not "he" or "she". Do you know who it was?'

'I couldn't tell. The voice was soft and sort of whispered my name.'

'And where were you during this episode?'

'I'd hidden in the bathroom. The policeman I spoke to told me to go there.'

'Are you on your own at present?'

'Sam's come over, so no, I have some company.'

'We'll come over later. I'll see the report first from the chaps who called. Stay where you are and we'll see you in a while.'

'Did you get the note I left in the office?' she asked.

'Yes, we did, thanks. I don't think it's significant at all. But thank you for keeping it.'

She hung up the phone. Sam went to look at the window catch while they were waiting. He tried to put it back together but had no luck.

'Damn it. I think we'll have to get a new one and I'm not sure how I can fix it.'

'Perhaps I should get a manufacturer to come and look at it?'

'That could take ages. I'll try to fix it somehow so at least you're safe.'

'You don't think they'll come back, do you?'

'Who knows? If they are desperate enough, they might. Have you got anyone who could come and stay with you?'

'Not really.'

'I suppose I could stay for a day or two.'

'That's very kind of you but I don't want to put you to any trouble. And I've only got one bedroom. It would have to be the couch.'

'Looks comfortable enough. Right. Well, I'll go back to my place and pick up a few things and come back. I'll bring something to fix the window too.'

'That's very good of you. But you'd better wait till the police have been. The DI said they'd come round later.'

'So who do you think it was?' asked the Detective Inspector.

'I know it isn't much help and it is only my opinion, but I feel it might have been Mr Johnson or Mrs Smith. They both knew Mr Baldwin from the past and both seemed to know about his work. Then it was Mr Johnson who was arguing with the Miss Christophers, wasn't it? He had walked along the cliff and was seen arguing. Perhaps they'd challenged him and perhaps he gave them a shove. Sorry, this is my imagination. I didn't see any of that. And he did go away quite quickly, didn't he?'

'And do you have any thoughts along these lines, Sam?'

'I have no idea. I wasn't quite as involved with the guests as Demelza. What she says is quite likely, though. Oh, and don't forget the Quickes. Has anything been heard of them?'

'We have traced them. Evidently their mother, or one of their mothers, was taken ill and they called a taxi early, during the night. It looks as though they are in the clear.'

'Goodness me. They might have left a message for us or something.'

'Well, it was the middle of the night. No, I think they are innocent. We'll bear in mind what you have told us. And you think it could have been one of the two parties who broke in here?'

'I suppose so. I think it might have been Mr Johnson who wanted to make sure I hadn't heard anything more.'

'Very well. We'll be off then. I'll keep in touch and don't worry. A patrol car will drive round during the night and keep a watch on this place. Can you get the window repaired?' She looked at Sam.

'I think I can probably fix it, assuming I can get a new catch. Trouble is, these plastic windows can easily be damaged. I'm going to come and stay here for a day or two till we know she's safe again.'

DI Black nodded and he and the Detective Constable left.

'Do you think he believed me?' she asked.

'I really don't know. Look, I'll go to the DIY store on my way and see what I can find. Will you be all right?'

'Of course. I do need to get some shopping but I'll wait till you're back. I can do that while you work on the window. Thanks so much, Sam. It is kind of you.'

'Not at all. Besides, it does give us the chance to get to know each other a little better.'

By the middle of the afternoon, they were drinking coffee, with a mended window catch and a stew simmering slowly on the cooker. The phone rang.

'It's Sadie Baldwin here. How are you?'

'Oh, Sadie. Lovely to hear from you. How are you getting on?'

'I've decided to return to the US of A. There's little to be achieved from staying here so I've booked my flight for tomorrow. I wanted to thank you for all your kindness. Fortunately I had your cell phone number in mine so thought I'd give you a call.'

'That's very kind of you. Sam is here with me. He says hi.' Sam had nodded his agreement to her comment.

'I always knew you were a couple. I wish you all the best. Poor Hermie will be shipped over later when the police are done with him. Anyway, many thanks to you.'

'Not at all. I'm just so sorry it happened. I'm glad the police have said you can go home.'

'Oh, but they haven't. Don't say anything to them, please. They don't even know I'm going.'

'Oh, I see. I hope that's wise.' She paused expecting some sort of answer. 'Well, have a safe trip back home.'

'Thank you, dear. Goodbye, then.'

'Goodbye, Sadie.' She switched off her phone. 'That was so nice of her, wasn't it? She's going back home tomorrow. Poor Sadie. I'm not sure how she'll cope on her own.'

'She's quite tough, actually. I shouldn't feel sorry for her. I think she'll cope very well.'

'What do you mean?'

'I don't know. Just something about her.' Sam was thoughtful.

'But she was a dreadful state the morning it happened. And she certainly wasn't with the group when the two old ladies went off the cliff.' Sam gave a shrug. 'What? You don't think she could have done it, do you?'

'Not pushed the old ladies over certainly, but she could easily have bumped off her husband.'

Demelza stared at her friend. She was amazed that he could even think that Sadie could be guilty.

'I don't think you could be right. She was so upset. And there was the business of the lost key and well, I really don't think it's possible. I'm sorry but you're wrong.'

'Maybe. If she's going home tomorrow, they'll need to decide quickly if she did do it. I suppose she's told them she's leaving?'

'Well, no. She says not. She asked me not to tell them.' She gave a shrug. 'No use speculating. We have to get on with our lives. Now, how about that casserole? I think it must be done by now.'

They spent a pleasant evening, chatting about their lives apart from Poldark. When it reached ten-thirty, they both yawned.

'I think I'm about ready for some sleep,' Sam announced.

'I'll get you some blankets. Are you sure you'll be all right on the sofa?'

'I've got a sleeping bag and yes, I'm sure I'll be fine. I really don't think there'll be any trouble but I'll stay on just in case.'

'I don't like to be a helpless woman, but I am grateful. Until they've actually caught someone, I do feel a bit vulnerable.'

'Well, I'm here for now, so stop worrying. I could do with a pillow if you have a spare?'

'Of course. I'll get one. And thank you again for being here. I do appreciate it.'

After a further cup of chocolate and more chatter, he settled down and Demelza went to her room. She felt totally shattered and soon fell asleep. This time she was not awakened during the night and slept on peacefully until eight o'clock. She stiffened as she heard noises coming from the other room and remembered Sam was there. She shot out of bed and pulled on her dressing gown. He was in the kitchen making coffee.

'Sorry. I should be doing that.'

'Hope you don't mind. Couldn't wait any longer. How did you sleep?'

'Wonderfully well, thank you. Made such a difference knowing you were here. How about you?'

'Not too bad. Actually, not really very well. There's a spring in your sofa that definitely needs attention.'

'Oh dear. I am sorry. I suppose I need a new sofa but it is on the list, somewhere after several other things.'

They had breakfast and were trying to decide what to do with their day when her mobile rang.

'Hallo?'

'It's DI Black. Just thought I'd let you know we've caught Wilf Johnson and he's in custody. He won't admit to murdering Hermie but he's finally given in and admitted to giving Miss Christopher a push. He insists it wasn't intended as murder but she slipped and then fell. The other one was so keen to try to save her sister, she also slipped and fell down. That's his story anyway and he's been charged. Thought it might help you if I phoned you.'

'Goodness, what a time you've had. But thank you so much for letting me know. Was it him who broke into my flat? You sound certain about his involvement with Hermie's death?'

'He is adamant about that. Swears he had nothing to do with it. We'll keep asking him for the next twenty-four hours and longer if necessary. I'll ask him about breaking in. I think you might be right about that one.'

'You do know that Sadie is returning to the States today?'

'No, I didn't know. She begged to be allowed to leave but I said not yet. We haven't really finished with her yet. Thanks for letting me know. I'll see about getting her flight stopped. Better go. I'll say goodbye then. Take care.'

'DI Black, I take it?' Sam asked.

'He says he's charging Mr Johnson for the murder of the Christophers. He's claiming it was all an accident and he didn't mean to kill them. He swears he didn't kill Hermie, though. They are still working on that. Perhaps he didn't kill him. I dunno.'

'I thought she said not to tell him about her leaving?'

'Oh goodness. Me and my big mouth. He's going to try to stop her going. Oh dear. She'll know it was me who split on her.'

'Let's go for a long walk. Clear our heads. Don't worry, love. You've probably done them a favour.'

Chapter Eleven

Mr Johnson had been collected from his home a few miles away and brought to Cornwall, where he was being interviewed.

'Come on now, Mr Johnson. You've already told us you knew Hermie before you went on this trip.'

'Yes, but only through work. Mrs Smith also knew him. We did a deal with his company ages ago. It was a surprise when they turned up on this bloody trip. I can't tell you how much I regret going on it in the first place.'

'You've admitted being present when the Miss Christophers went over the cliff.'

'I've told you all that.' He assumed the sort of patience as if he was speaking to a sub-intelligent child. 'She was accusing me of murdering Hermie and I got mad and pushed her away from me. Surely that must count as an accident? The first one went over the cliff and the second fell over looking for her sister.'

'And the break-in at Demelza's place?'

'I've told you again and again. It wasn't me. I don't even know where the woman lives. Why on earth would I go there anyway?'

'You tell me.' He remained silent. 'All right. Tell me about your connection to Maggie Smith.'

'Like I said. We'd met at a conference when we were both trying to get him to agree to a deal. Our company won and Maggie left with her tail between her legs. Perhaps you should be asking *her* why *she* bumped him off.' He folded his arms and sat back in his seat. 'Look, could I have a coffee, please?' he asked.

'Constable? Can you organise him a coffee?'

'Sir,' he murmured as he left the room.

'Come on now, Mr Johnson. Admit it now and save yourself a whole lot of trouble later.'

'I won't admit to doing something I didn't do. I've admitted to one load of trouble but I'm standing firm. I swear to you, I did not kill Hermie Baldwin.'

'Why did you drive away from the café site? You ordered a taxi but then you went in another car.'

'I phoned a work colleague who happened to be holidaying down here. Just to tell him what had happened, you understand. He took it on himself to drive over to collect me. I could hardly turn him down now, could I?'

'I don't see why not. It caused a lot of speculation and you must admit, it made you look guilty. You say you were involved with the deaths of these two ladies and you, evidently, wanting to escape so hurriedly, what else can we think?'

'It was an accident. I keep telling you that. I want a solicitor. I'm not going to answer any more of your questions.'

'Very well, sir. Do you have a solicitor in mind?'

'Oh, goodness me. My chap is miles away. It'll take him half a day to get here.'

'We can provide the duty solicitor.'

'Okay then. That'll have to do. Obviously I need someone on my side.'

The constable came back with a plastic cup of coffee and a couple of packs of sugar. He dumped it down on the desk in front of Wilf. DI Black nodded at him.

'He wants the duty solicitor. I'll leave you with your coffee and give him a call.'

The two of them left him, locking the door behind them. He looked at a list and dialled a number.

'Could the duty solicitor come to the station, please? Yes, someone needs him.'

Half an hour later a smart, rather hard-looking woman arrived.

'Sarah Bayliss. You've got a case for me?'

'Come on through. DI Black is in charge of this case. I'll give him a call,' said the duty sergeant.

DI Black quickly put her in the picture about the case and showed her through to the prisoner.

'Best of luck with him.' He opened the door and announced, 'This is Ms Bayliss. I'll leave you with her to sort out your defence.' He left the room and the two occupants began their interview. Half an hour later, Ms Bayliss came out of the room and found DI Black.

'Seems to me you have the person who caused the accident that led to the deaths of the Misses Christopher. I don't think there's a shred of evidence to charge him with the murder of ... what was his name? Oh yes, Mr Hermie Baldwin,' she said after consulting her notes. 'I suggest the charge against him for the deaths of the Christophers can stand but he will defend himself against murder. It will probably be involuntary manslaughter he could be charged with. As for the other murder, you need to keep looking. I really do believe he is innocent of that one.'

'What about the break-in to Demelza's house or flat or whatever it is?'

'Okay, I suppose he is guilty of that. He told me he wanted to talk to her to see what they knew and what might happen with the police. I don't think there was any intent to harm her.'

'That's as may be. But he terrified the life out of her. He did say he didn't know where she lived.'

'Yes, well he quickly found out from his office. He had access to a list of addresses.'

'We can add that one to his charges. All right, well, thank you very much for being so honest.'

Later that day, Wilf was imprisoned pending a bail hearing. He was not a happy man and pleaded his innocence as he was taken out of the police station.

'I don't get on with women. I need a male solicitor. Find me one. Who's going to tell my wife? And my business will all go to the dogs.' Still protesting violently, he was taken to the cell to await the prison van.

'I suppose our next move is to Heathrow,' DI Black said to his sergeant, somewhat resignedly.

'I suppose we do have to go there? Couldn't she be brought here to us?'

'It's a case of whether or not we shall charge her. I find it hard to believe she's guilty. She was so upset about his death. But, she's about to disappear back to America somewhat against our orders.'

'Perhaps her reaction was all just an act.'

'Maybe. I'll see if there's someone who can bring her to Cornwall. Don't suppose she'll be particularly pleased and if she is innocent, we shall then have to take her back to Heathrow.'

'I suppose you're right. But frankly, I'm bushed. I really need some sleep.'

'I'll agree to getting her brought here. You go and get to bed. We'll interview her tomorrow.'

Protesting violently, Sadie Baldwin was driven back to Cornwall. She had expected being almost back in the States by now and that wretched detective had sent for her again. She moaned once they were on their way and scarcely stopped complaining throughout the journey. The DI had organised a place for her to stay in a bed and breakfast place near the police station. This did not please her either and she demanded a better hotel. Nobody listened to her. As it was fairly late when she arrived, she finally agreed to settle down and apparently tossed around for most of the night.

'I really do not appreciate this treatment,' she announced the next morning. 'Why on earth did you stop me from leaving? And to dump me in that awful B & B. You'll be hearing from our solicitors.'

'I'm sorry, Mrs Baldwin. It is unfortunate that you were trying to leave without our permission.'

'Your permission? Your permission? How dare you? It sounds as if you think me guilty of something. It was my own dear darling husband who was murdered in a most horrible way. I shall never forget the amount of blood that flowed from him. It was truly horrible.'

'I do understand that. As soon as we have made our decision, you will be free to leave.'

'So I should think. I trust you will then drive me back to Heathrow as soon as possible.'

'If you would come into the interview room. Do you want a solicitor?'

'Why on earth should I want one of those leeches?'

'I'm merely offering you the chance.'

'You can't possibly think I'm guilty. Let's get this over with, so I can get back on my way home. This sort of behaviour could never happen in the States.'

Sadie Baldwin seemed a very different person to the crying miserable woman he'd seen at the hotel. She now seemed so much stronger and much more positive. DI Black was struck by the thought that she could possibly have committed the murder herself. He had resisted the thought till now, to avoid any prejudice and had tried to push it to the back of his mind.

'Take a seat,' he offered when they reached the interview room. She slumped down into the chair and sat looking very angry. He switched on the tape recorder. 'Twenty-ninth of September. Nine-thirty a.m. Interview with Mrs Sadie Baldwin. DI Black and DC Thompson present. I'd like to go through that morning at the Poldark Lodge Hotel. Tell me exactly what happened, please.'

'Oh, for goodness' sakes. I really don't want to live through it all again. I told you what happened. I woke up to find myself covered in blood and Hermie lying there, dead.' She spoke angrily and seemed quite fierce.

'You said at the time there was someone in the room with you.'

'Did I? Well, that's how it must have been.'

'Do you mean you can't remember, or that there wasn't anyone there?'

'Look, it's all like a bad dream to me.' She paused and went quiet for a moment as if she was remembering. 'I'm sorry. I really can't cope with all this.' Tears began to flow again and she dabbed her eyes. The DC looked at his boss who nodded. He reached for a box of tissues and passed them to Sadie.

'I'm sorry,' the Detective Inspector said softly. 'I know it's a dreadful experience for you but you must understand why we need to ask you these questions.' She sniffed hard and nodded.

'Okay. You ask away.'

'Let's go back to the someone in the room. What can you remember about them?'

'It was just a shape. I couldn't say who it was. They walked past the bed and out of the door. I sat up and spoke to Hermie, only he was dead. I then leapt up, positively leapt out of bed and ran to the door. I went into the corridor and then I think I must have yelled. "*He's dead ... someone's killed him*" or words to that effect. Then it all started happening. People came and surrounded me and took me to the lounge. Or wherever it was.'

'You said a torch was flashed in your eyes. What can you remember about that?'

'Did I? I suppose that must be what happened, then.'

'You also said you tried to put the lights on but they didn't work.'

'Did I? That's what must have happened. It's all become blurry. I honestly can't remember what I said. If I said the lights didn't work, than that's what happened.'

'Yet when the SOCOs went in, all the lights worked perfectly.'

'Oh, I don't know. Perhaps I just fumbled and couldn't make them work. I've told you. I really can't remember exactly what happened.'

'I think you can, Mrs Baldwin. I suspect you're pretending to be confused. Trying to make yourself look innocent.'

'But don't you see? I am innocent. I loved Hermie. Everyone loved Hermie. I can't think of anyone who hated him enough to do this terrible thing to him.'

'You said you've been married for three years?'

'That's right.'

'Not so very long, is it?'

'We were both married before but it didn't work out. Then we met and fell in love and it was all straightforward from then on.' Tears rose again in her eyes and she started to sob again.

'Come on now. You really don't need to start that again.'

'You are heartless. You simply don't understand my terrible loss.' She reached for another tissue and bent her head to sob some more. 'You simply don't understand.'

'You're probably right. Did you kill your husband?' he threw in largely to shock her. She looked at him in surprise and hesitated for a moment before starting a new, huge burst of crying.

'How could you? How could you think that?'

'I don't know. I simply don't know. It just seems a possibility. I think the figure you claim to have seen, well, that was just a figment of your imagination. I don't for a moment think he or she really existed. I put it to you, things were not how you saw them. You decided to kill Hermie to see what you could get out of his estate. I think you're a scheming, hard woman who was simply out for what you could get.' He leaned back after his speech and waited for it to have an impact.

His DC sat staring at him. Where had all that come from? He then looked at Mrs Baldwin to see the effect it had on her. She had paled and looked totally pathetic. Her mouth had dropped open in shock. Then she drew in a deep breath, her colour flooded back into her face and she seemed to grow in size.

'How dare you? How dare you speak to me like that?' Her eyes narrowed and she seemed to be positively incandescent. 'You suggested I might need a lawyer. I need one here, right now.'

'We'll call the duty solicitor. Keeping her rather busy at the moment. But, you haven't given me an answer. Did you kill your husband?'

'I refuse to answer anything else without an attorney present.' She folded her arms and sat with her mouth clamped shut.

'Can you call the lawyer, DC Thompson?' He switched off the recording device and the two of them rose and left the room. Sadie Baldwin sat sobbing.

'I say, sir, you were pushing it a bit, weren't you?' said DC Thompson, when they were outside the room.

'I suppose so. Think it was the last lot of wailing that did it for me. I lost my rag a bit. Still, it did pay off. She couldn't answer me. I think that is pretty conclusive proof that she's as guilty as hell.'

'I wish I could share your optimism. She may be guilty but I fear it's going to be tricky to prove.'

They went to the office and the lawyer was called. She arrived a few minutes later and they told her what had happened. It was the same Ms Bayliss who had attended Wilf Johnson the previous day.

'Is this the same case?' she asked.

'She is the wife of the murdered man. I'm afraid I just accused her of carrying out the crime.' The solicitor scowled. 'No, I don't have any proof and was using my intuition. Anyway, I'll show you through to her.'

'Thank you. I'll see you later but I must tell you, I do not approve of your accusation.' The detective gave a shrug and opened the interview room to let Ms Bayliss go in to meet her latest client. It was about half an hour later that she came out. She looked somewhat less confident than when she went in.

'How did that go?' asked DI Black.

'No comment. If you're now ready to continue the interview?'

'I'll call my colleague and join you in there.'

The next half an hour proved very frustrating, as all Mrs Baldwin would say was 'no comment'. The detective glared at the solicitor who had given her this advice. She in turn shrugged.

'We'll keep her in overnight and speak again tomorrow. Perhaps a day of reflection will persuade her to say something,' the inspector said. He looked at Mrs Baldwin, who refused to meet his gaze. 'Come along. I'll show you to your er, room.' He took her along to one of the holding cells and was about to lock her in when she spoke again.

'I need my handbag. Do you think you could get it for me?' she asked.

'Sorry, no. There's a blanket in there and that's it.'

'But this is unpardonable. You're treating me like a prisoner.' He gave a shrug as he left her. She could spend the time thinking, and tomorrow they would see how she behaved. Next on his agenda was the bail hearing for Mr Johnson. What a messy business it all was. His case was put and the redoubtable Ms Bayliss fought for the prisoner and won. He was released on bail.

DI Black went home early and was sitting quietly watching something he knew not what, when his phone rang.

'I think you should come down to the station, sir. It's Mrs Baldwin.'

'What about Mrs Baldwin?'

'She's tried to kill herself. It's touch and go. The ambulance has been called but you'll need to see her, sir.'

'On my way,' he sighed. Bloody woman, he was thinking. How on earth had she tried to kill herself? She had nothing in the cell with her, damn it.

'So, how did she do it?' he demanded when he arrived at the station.

'It seems she had some poison hidden somewhere. She was unconscious when we found her.'

'Good lord. Sounds pretty desperate. Do we have any idea why?'

'Not really. Guilty of the crime she's been arrested for?'

'Maybe. So where is she now?'

'The ambulance team have taken her to Treliske. I somehow doubt she's going to make it.'

'Right. Well, I suppose I'd better go to Treliske.' He was halfway there when he received a phone call.

'Sorry, sir,' said the duty sergeant. 'Mrs Baldwin's just died. You may as well give up on her.'

'Thanks, Bill. I'll go back home again. See you in the morning.' It looked as if his potentially guilty customer was now out of the picture. He cursed himself for not putting her in one of their boiler suits, but she was only being held on suspicion. Perhaps if she have been given some paper and pencil, she might have written a note to explain things. He would speak to Ms Bayliss the following day and see if she had anything to say about the woman. Fingers crossed, Mrs Baldwin may have confessed all to this solicitor.

DI Black was early the next morning. He felt somewhat frustrated about his suspect. He chatted it over with his DC and they both came to the same conclusion. She must have been guilty and felt they were getting too close.

'I'll call Ms Bayliss and see what she's got to say,' DI Black decided.

'I suppose if she's dead there's no reason the keep it from you,' she told him. 'She did finally admit to me that it was she had done the deed. This was when she said "*no comment*" all the time. She felt their marriage was actually on dodgy ground and knew she would inherit his money if he died quickly. He'd already re-written his will, actually, we've discovered. A sad case.'

'My goodness, yes. She put up an incredible performance. She was about to leave the country when we stopped her and called her back for interview. All the same, it was a terrible way to go.'

'Well, thank you for your honesty. You'll be called at the inquest, of course.'

'And of course, there's Mr Johnson. I'll be acting for him at his trial.'

'Indeed. Let's hope he doesn't try anything stupid in the meantime. It was still him who broke into Demelza's flat.'

'You may be right. But I don't think you'll have too much trouble with him. He is prepared to fight.'

'Hmm, yes. Thanks for your time, Ms Bayliss. Goodbye.'

'I think that about does our investigation. Now all there is to do are the reports.'

'What about Demelza and Sam?'

'Perhaps you can give them a call. They've been very helpful. They will, of course, be asked to attend the inquest. You could tell them that.'

He settled down in his chair and began to write his reports. Another case was solved but it left him feeling somewhat frustrated. He gave a sigh and powered up his computer.

Epilogue

When they found out what had happened, Sam and Demelza were rather saddened and she actually felt slightly guilty.

'She really took us in, didn't she?' Sam commented.

'I now feel sort of guilty at the time I spent sympathising with Sadie Baldwin. She certainly put on a good show of bereaved widow and I fell for it, hook, line and sinker. All the same, it's so sad to think of her killing herself. I really can't believe any of it is worthwhile. All for money, too. Amazing what that does to a person.'

Sam listened to her and told her, 'You were doing your job and being sympathetic was a part of that. I thought you were magnificent, actually.' She blushed.

'Aw, thanks. I hope I was some use at the time.'

'I think you were. Demelza, I really want to get to know you much better. I feel there could be a future for us.' He reached over to her and took her hand.

'Really? I feel pretty much the same.'

They kissed for the first time and certainly not the last.

Printed in Great Britain
by Amazon